VICTORIA

VICTORIA

FRANCES HENDRY

Hodder
Children's
Books

A division of Hodder Headline Limited

From the author

England in 61CE, during the Roman occupation and Boudicca's rebellion, was a dangerous, violent, often brutally terrifying place. Blood and death were never far away, and hard choices often had to be made; not between good and bad, but between bad and worse. People had to be tough, strong, brave – and lucky – just to stay alive. Thousands didn't. Friendship could make all the difference between living and dying.

Yes, it was harsh. I've tried to reflect this world for people of today without glamorising it, or skirting the realities, or wallowing in gore. But to my character, Victoria, it was reality.

Thanks to Dr Jenny Hall, of the Museum of London, for kindly checking the Roman facts for me; to Catherine Fisher for advice about the Celtic background; to my friend Mary Grosvenor, my daughter Jenny, and the Nairn librarians for information about assorted odd subjects; and to my husband Alex for innumerable cups of tea.

Frances Mary Hendry

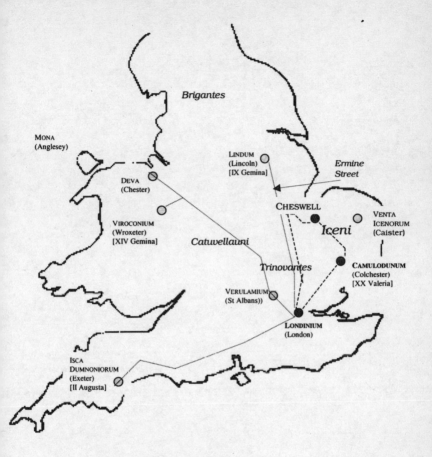

Places in 'Boudicca'

○ - - Victoria's Journey   ⋯⋯⋯ Roman road

   Settlement mentioned; LATIN/CELTIC NAME (modern name) [Legion stationed
● there]

   Settlement where Victoria stayed.

Most common tribe in area.

[Not to scale; there were other towns and roads]

I

The sword knocked aside Victoria's parry, slid past her shield and stabbed into her ribs. Though she tried not to act like a girl, she couldn't quite stop a grunt, in spite of Dio's thick old army tunic. However, in a carpenter's yard the clacking of wood wasn't unusual, and half drowned anyway by the smithy next door.

She straightened painfully. 'Better!' Dio approved her. 'Stayed alive almost long enough to run away! But you got to control that temper! You lose control, slash wild, your man can duck past your sword an' get you. An' keep up them wrist exercises, eh? You'll end up one o' them female gladiators we hear about in Rome, eh?'

'A gladiator? Don't even joke about it!' Victoria exclaimed. Ordinary slaves, even kitchen skivvies, swineherds, tanners stinking from the urine pits, looked down on gladiators. The men who fought in the arena were also slaves, but often murderers or ex-soldiers, bought by trainers after brutal crimes; the lowest of the low. And gladiatrixes must be even worse; vicious, ugly hags for sure – who else would descend so low?

Dio laughed at her disgust. 'Don't sneer, lass, they ain't all bad. I trained for a while ten year back, wi' Bombio, in Massilia.

Not as good as Capua, where the best trainers are, but not bad neither. Ran an evenin' class for likely lads like me. Temptin', too. Contract yourself wi' a trainer, just for twenty or thirty fights, for a chance o' glory and fame, presents, fancy dinners, all the girls after you, big prizes – sounded good, eh? Mars Ultor, you could do well under Caligula, or Claudius – if you lived! Even that old miser Tiberius paid a thousand gold pieces for a single appearance by a champion! But me mum said she'd murder me, so I joined the cavalry instead. Thirty year to serve, but Roman citizenship an' a pay-off an' land at the end.'

Victoria grinned. 'Better than dying in the arena?'

'Aye, lass. Better chance o' survivin', too. See, I'm here, ain't I, eh? Even wi' this hand off, as the legion funeral club paid me well for.' With the hook that replaced his left hand he reached to snag his tunic from a post, and wiped his sweaty face with it before pulling it on over his trousers. 'Whoo! I had the slimmest waist in the troop, me horse thought he were carryin' a feather, and look at me! Turnin' into a tub o' lard I am, lass, runnin' the yard here for your dad ain't keepin' me slim, no way! This jiggin' about's doin' me the world o' good.'

Watching from the side, old Bron's pouchy face was twisted in his usual fussy disapproval. 'Women fighting! Disgraceful! Immodest!'

'I'm half Iceni, and mother says lots of Iceni women learn to fight, there are even women warriors. She approves!' Victoria snapped at the old slave.

2

'Master wouldn't!' His face was doleful as a bloodhound. 'If he ever finds out, he'll sell me.'

'Maybe you'd be happier with another owner!' Bron glowered, and Victoria cursed herself. Her temper again! Certainly they'd all be happier if Father sold Bron, but it would never happen. Besides, if she upset the old clerk too much, he might just decide that snitching on her would save him punishment for allowing her scandalous unwomanly pastime to go on for so long – almost five months now, ever since the spring. Since he'd arrived by chance one day while she was practising, he came along most days for a few minutes to watch; rather enviously, she thought, though he couldn't admit it. Calm him down . . . 'Don't worry, Bron, Father couldn't run the business without you. Besides, he won't find out.' Her stare challenged him. 'Who'd tell him?'

'Cheer up, old misery-guts!' Dio slapped Bron's shoulder. 'My lads'll keep quiet about this prank if they know what's good for 'em, nor we can't be seen from outside, an' the lass never squawks when she's hit – a right warrior, eh?'

Snorting contempt at the flattery, Victoria still flushed with pleasure.

'Whoo! Enough!' Dio tossed her his sword. 'I'm meltin', lass, put these away. We'll get you up on a horse again tomorrow.'

'Oh, Mars! Do I have to?' She hated riding. Stupid smelly big brute jouncing her about, stubborn, malicious!

3

'Yes! You want to learn to fight, you'll get taught proper! An' that means ridin'.'

She sighed, but she had to humour him. 'Noon again? Right. And thanks, Dio.'

He grinned. 'You'll do it yet, lass! Off home wi' you now before you're missed.'

'Missed?' Father paid her little heed, especially nowadays, since baby Rufinus was born. And Mother didn't care, as long as she did her housework, and a reasonable share of the eternal spinning. Victoria grimaced but nodded, tugged off the stinky padded shirt and laid the wooden swords out of sight on top of a stack of roughly squared logs.

'Aye, best be off home, young mistress.' Bron heaved himself to his feet, his joints creaking. 'Drogo's ship's just in with pottery, an' all to be checked for breakage. Drogo drives his crews too hard an' fast. I'd best get down to the river.' He heaved a hard-done-to sigh.

Victoria winked at Dio. 'Well, Bron, who else can Father trust?'

'True, true.' Bron's lips twitched in a sour nearly-smile. 'He needs me, that's true; into everything, he is. There's money in the town these days, nineteen shops now, for the builders an' traders an' legion wives, as well as the pubs an' workshops, an' the tribes growing civilised, even your mother's Iceni, wanting their oil an' wine an' fish sauce, an' he'll have his share! He'll be buying his own ships soon, not hiring. Quick as you can drilling them water-pipes, Dio, the master's promised them for the new houses they're starting up the west end. More work . . . Ha, well. Somebody's got to do it, an' always the same folk.' He grumbled off, happily martyred.

Grinning, Victoria pulled her tucked-up gown from her belt, smoothed it, and rinsed her face and bruised knuckles at the water-trough. 'See you tomorrow, Dio.'

The main road along the slope above the river was busy, as usual. Londinium already held about eight thousand people, not counting the farmers round about, and was growing fast, with bankers and moneychangers from all over the Empire, from Turkey to Africa to – well, to here. When her father was invalided out of the Second Augusta Legion four years before, he had taken his retirement grant of land here, near his old contacts and cronies, and his trading profits were proving him right. He was even talking about building a stone house soon, the first in the town, like the ones away over the Narrow Sea in Rome. Though the Procurator, Emperor Nero's money man in charge of taxes and paying the army and so on, had a bath in his house up in the army camp, even his offices were wood and plaster.

Just ahead of Victoria, some boys were shouting: Gallus, and that big bully Myron, and three mates, impatient to join the army next year when they were sixteen and Mars-cursed nuisances in the meantime. She strode on defiantly; she'd not dodge those louts.

They were jeering at a smaller boy with a crutch, a native, backed up against a shed. 'Gimpy!' 'Bet he's a slave!' 'Who'd buy him?' 'Hey, short-leg, why don't you run away? That's what dirty tribesmen always do!' The boy's face was bleeding, his checked trousers and tunic torn, his hooded cloak dashed with muck and dung. They must have tripped or pelted him, but he faced and cursed them bravely.

At least he had the sense not to draw his knife. The Second Augusta had moved its headquarters west, but there was always one cohort of about eight hundred men based up at the old camp here to police the new jetties and streets, and protect the Procurator and his clerks. A patrol was lounging in the open front of a tavern across the street, officially on duty though their helmets and shields were piled casually against a wall. She knew their leader, Certinus, the optio or second-in-command of the cohort's second century, a tough, experienced young soldier; not one to let a local lad off lightly if he dared harm a Roman.

'The Morrigan rip your worm-eaten guts out and feed them to the ravens!' the lad yelled.

Victoria blinked; she understood what he was saying. This boy wasn't from a local tribe, as she had assumed, but Iceni, one of her mother's tribe up north. She knew quite a bit from speaking to Mother, though it was always Latin when Father was home, of course.

Her ready temper suddenly flared.

Though stern, her father was usually even-tempered, but every few months, if something outside upset him, he beat her and her mother for the slightest cause. Just like these bullies, he'd suddenly storm, 'Dirty savages! Uncivilised brutes! Horus curse this god-forsaken country, cold and wet and dark and not a drop of decent wine, and full of brainless, clumsy barbarians like you!' And his fists and belt thudding . . .

Mother said they must respect and obey him as the head of the house, and just be glad he didn't hit the younger girls. Glad? Huh!

But Victoria didn't have to respect and obey Gallus and Myron!

A water carrier was passing, two empty wooden buckets on his yoke. Victoria tapped his arm, said politely, 'Excuse me, let me borrow this,' lifted the sturdy spar from the man's shoulders, swung it round her head hard, and slung it right into the bullies' backs.

One fell instantly, half stunned by a whirling bucket; Gallus yelled in outrage as the yoke slammed into his back, knocking him to his knees; and a third screamed as the other bucket smashed his elbow, knocking a stone from his hand.

The Iceni lad gaped at the tall, lithe girl storming to his rescue, her red hair flying. Shrieking involuntarily, Victoria dodged a blow from Myron and, as he kicked at her, grabbed his foot and heaved. With a satisfying thud and screech he crashed on his back, while the Iceni boy, yelling a joyous war-cry, stabbed the last oaf in the belly with his crutch, grabbed his ears as he folded and sank his teeth into the lout's nose.

Myron staggered to his feet and started to draw a knife, but the legionaries, guffawing like jackasses, had recognised Victoria and roused themselves to close in.

'Enough, Myron, stop there! Well done, Vicky! Myron, draw that and I'll have your guts for bootlaces,' Certinus snapped. 'Beaten, five of you, by a girl and a kid! Puny chickens!' His squad agreed. They rescued the half-chewed bully, hauled the others to their feet and urged them home, heavy hob-nailed legion boots helping Myron on his way when he tried to argue.

'Want to join up, lad? You've a fine spirit!' Certinus reached to clap the Iceni boy on the shoulder, but the youngster ducked silently away from the friendly hand, wiping his mouth. 'No Latin? Pity. Not with that short leg, neither. But don't need cannibals, do we, eh, Vicky? Mars Ultor, what a girl – we could do with you to put some spirit into the troops!'

Panting as her rage died, Victoria bumped him up a rank, to be polite. 'Thank you, Centurion.'

Certinus snorted. 'Want to bring me bad luck, girl?'

'Bad luck?'

'Centurion of the second century's retiring soon, girl,' a soldier explained, chuckling. 'So all the centurions move up, right? So our optimistic optio here's hoping he'll be promoted to the empty spot in the sixth century, and get his very own

8

ash stick to wallop us poor squaddies with! But don't call him centurion yet!'

Victoria touched iron to counter her unlucky words. The gods could be offended, and stop Certinus' promotion, just out of spite at her taking them and the future for granted. 'Oh, I'm sorry! Fortuna bring you your promotion, Optio Certinus! And thank you for helping us.'

'Helping *him*, you mean, *you* didn't need it!' He grinned down at her. 'Hey, tell your dad to get in fast and he'll be on to a good thing at Isca Dumnoniorum, the legion's main fort, you know? Out west where we fought under General Vespasian during the invasion. The legate's gone home on family business, and the acting commander wants a whole new set of tableware – says the camp stuff must have come over with Vespasian, it's so chipped! Snooty swine! So, since your dad's an old mate . . .'

Eagerly, Victoria nodded. This would be a good sale! 'Yes, Optio, he'll be happy to supply you. We've a new cargo just arrived, top quality. He'll come up to the camp tomorrow to talk to the quartermaster. Thank you again!'

'Thanks to you for the show, Vicky! Best fight since that bear killed three dogs last year, remember it?' Chuckling, the soldiers strolled back to their ale. The water-carrier had already hurried off.

Victoria was left staring at the boy she had rescued, not knowing quite what to do next. He was small and thin, with big dark-blue eyes and a neat, prim mouth; good-looking apart

9

from ears that stuck out through his long fair hair like amphora handles, and that bad leg, wizened and twisted under the cross-bindings of his trousers.

To her surprise, he suddenly spoke in accented but reasonably correct Latin. 'Thanks to you, girl. Am I right – are you Boudicca?'

Victoria blinked. 'I thought you didn't know Latin? Speak Iceni if you like, Mother taught me. No, I'm not Boudicca, I'm Victoria.'

The lad nodded. 'It is the same name, after Bouda, goddess of victory. Like Boudicca, chief wife of our chief Prasutaeg. You are the child of Mara, daughter of Cermona of the Iceni? If so, the gods have given us a happy meeting, for I was sent to fetch you.'

Oh, Mars – had someone told Father about her sword-fighting?

'Come, girl.' The boy turned regally away. Victoria nearly clipped his ear for him. Who did he think he was, giving her orders? Emperor Nero? But he might be a customer. And he was crippled, and hurt; he staggered as he turned. She reached to support him, but he shoved himself upright. 'I don't need help!'

Her temper flared again. 'All right! Fall, then!'

'I can manage!' The boy's bad leg was a full hand's-breadth shorter than the other, so that he had to lurch along. Suddenly his crutch slipped on a muddy stone and he half fell to sit on a step, luckily behind a stall, out of sight of the soldiers. 'Don't touch me!' He huddled in on himself, shuddering, flinching from sympathy.

Victoria huffed. Arrogant little snit! But . . . she did the same herself, proudly trying to hide any hurt. And he'd been sent for her. And he called her Boudicca. Had she really the same name as the Iceni chief's principal wife? She hesitated, then squatted beside him, to hold out her hand and show that it was trembling. He glanced sideways at her. She nodded. 'It happens every time.' Apart from being true, it gave him an excuse for collapsing.

'Always? You are often in fights?'

She grinned. 'Only with Father.'

'Your father beats you?' The boy sounded shocked. 'If I do wrong, my father tells me how my behaviour has disgraced him. What more is needed? But,' he eyed her pityingly, 'you are reared as a Roman, and everybody knows Romans have no honour.'

'No honour? Of course we do!'

He shrugged. 'Your soldiers fight in armour, cowardly, afraid to die. They do not accept challenges to duel. They feel no shame to have their heads left on the battlefield.'

'Heads? You still take heads? In the old days, yes, but—'

'Old ways were good. If you do not please the gods with sacrifice, why should they favour you? Besides, you honour an enemy by displaying his head, to boast that you are a better

11

man. The Romans stop wars, demand peace, as if we were old women. Contemptible! But you, girl, you have courage. You are not entirely Roman. I'll make a song about you.'

'A song?' Victoria mentally shook herself. She sounded like a faulty echo. Was that a compliment? She got so few, she scarcely recognised it.

The boy gestured resignedly to his crippled leg. 'Three years ago this happened, when I was twelve.' He was the same age as she was, though much smaller. 'We were travelling, camped for the night, when our horses began screaming. We thought it was robbers, but it was a she-bear with two big cubs, and she grabbed my knee in her jaws. They move fast, you know.'

'I suppose so.' The agility of bears wasn't something she had really considered before.

'Father and mother speared them, of course, saved me, but . . .' He rubbed his knee resentfully, and the blue tattoo that ran up his neck and across one cheek. 'I have her fur on my bed, but . . . I can't kneel to drive a chariot, or balance in one like a warrior, fight with a sword or even ride a horse properly, so I'm going to Mona next spring – you know, the druids' island? – to train as a bard. It's not the same as being a warrior, but . . .'

She nodded. 'Mother says that has its own glory. Not in Rome – or even in Londinium! The Romans sneer at Emperor Nero, even, for singing in public. But Mother says among the tribes a king must honour any formal demand of a bard.'

'True.' He smiled, biting his lip. 'I already have a harp. She is named Larksong.'

Victoria climbed to her feet and again offered a hand. After a moment, he took it, and let her tug him up. 'By the way, who are you? You didn't tell me *your* name.'

He was taken aback. 'I'm sorry. Boudicca – no, Victoria, you say? Victoria, daughter of Mara, daughter of Cermona, I am Cram, son of Arvenic, son of Brinna, sister of Cermona. You are my third cousin. And you should also know that Cermona and Brinna were mother's sister's daughters to Prasutaeg, Chief Man of the Iceni.' He grinned at her bemused gaze. 'Yes, cousin. We are cousins to the king!'

II

As soon as they stepped up off the lane into Rufius Aegyptus's shop, Victoria and Cram could hear the voices from the back. Aegypta, Victoria's pretty second sister, minding the shop, was jumping with excitement. 'There you are! You've met him! He and his dad came in with silver – since King Prasutaeg died, that Roman senator who lent piles of silver to the Iceni nobles is demanding it all back right away, they're all hysterical about it! So our uncle brought some down here, to the procurator, to send safe to Rome under army escort with the tax money, and then they went for a drink and the tavern-keeper mentioned Mother as another of the Iceni. So they came to rescue her! Silly clots, as if we needed it!' She giggled and winked at Cram. 'Hello again, handsome! I could really fancy you, apart from that leg!'

Victoria raised an eyebrow. 'He speaks Latin.' Aegypta just giggled louder. 'You knew, didn't you? Light-skirt!' Victoria hissed, and beckoned Cram through into the rear of the house. To her relief, the young man's thin, intense face was wry but not upset; he must be used to this, she thought, and at least it was half a compliment. Trust Aegypta!

Proudly, she led Cram through the store-room, pointing

14

out Father's wares — stacked pottery and copper cooking pots and bowls, fat glazed amphorae of Spanish olives, tall wooden casks of German wine, scented boxes of spices and bags of herbs, fine table dishes crated in straw below the ladder up to the sleeping attic. 'Those glass bottles are scents and medicines, sent over by Father's relatives in Egypt. That's why he's called Aegyptus, of course. They cost at least a silver sesterce each!'

The big living-room behind was the brightest room she knew, even when the yard door was shut, for the window was large enough to need wooden bars for security, and the wide charcoal stove under it hadn't yet stained the new plaster with smoke. Mother had eight cooking pots of all sizes, from small sauce ones to one big enough to boil a whole goose. The private well under its lid in the corner was modern, too; every housewife in the street was badgering her husband to dig one.

A very tall, rangy tribesman in striped trousers and tunic, sleeveless wolfskin jerkin and bright chequered cloak half filled the room, his arms and neck ringed with heavy twisted gold above twisting tattoos and scars. He was holding Mother's hands and grinning like a bear. Though his long fair hair and moustache were plaited as a sign of peaceful intentions and tied with silver-tagged leather thongs, Mother was crying! But as Victoria stiffened, she realised it was from happiness, not fear.

15

Mara sniffed, wiping her eyes. 'This is my eldest, Victoria. Vicky, this is my mother's sister's son, your uncle Arvenic.'

'You never said your family were giants!' Victoria bit her lip. Her loose mouth!

Arvenic wasn't angry. He was complimented. He twirled the ends of his moustache with exaggerated conceit. 'The tallest man in the nine kingdoms!' he boasted, chuckling in an oddly high, light voice. 'Happy am I to meet you, my not-so-dwarf niece. Finding my lost cousin, and she well and happy, rich and honoured, with a fine family – this is double joy. We knew your mother was taken captive, and mourned her, thinking her dead or sold over the seas with so many others. I myself was wounded when we fought the Romans, left for dead. My wife Allis – you remember her, Mara? – she dragged me away and hid me. For two years I had to skulk about like a farmer, until the Romans calmed down. What relief, to wear my warrior's torc again, even though we may not carry our swords. You know that was why we fought, niece? Disarming us they planned to make us slaves, weevils gnaw their miserable little souls! And their taxes!'

'Enough misery, Arvenic! We must celebrate! A goose for dinner, as well as the pork stew, and we'll have herby dumplings, Rufius's favourites! And pears in spiced wine.'

Arvenic grinned, raising a mug of ale. 'Wine is thin stuff. We prefer this, Mara!'

'But not for stewing pears!' she scolded him, laughing. 'But yes, I make a good brew.' She called her small daughters. 'Rufinia! Finia, run get us another jugful, like a clever lass. Tilla, love, put down your dolly and fish me out a bowl of the best olives from the big jar in the store. Victoria, take out the axe to the fattest goose in the yard!'

While the girls were away, Mara told of being sold as a slave. 'It was – disgusting. But I had the luck to take the eye of a good man. Rufius Aegyptus was a quartermaster's clerk in the Second Augusta under General Vespasian, during Emperor Claudius's invasion when I was a child. Ah, good, Vicky, I'll pluck that, I'm quicker than you, you set the table – not the wood and horn, the best red-ware bowls and the bronze spoons! You see, Arvenic, when Rufius retired, I was bearing his child, so he freed me and married me. We had only daughters until recently – Victoria here, of course, Aegypta out in the shop, Rufinia and little Aegyptilla.' Beaming among a snowstorm of goose feathers, she gestured towards the cradle bobbing from a birch pole in the corner. 'But this is Rufinus Aegyptus, three months old, and two teeth already!'

The big man patted the baby's cheek with a finger as big as a sausage; 'May Lugh of the light bless you, little nephew. May you never know hunger nor thirst, cold nor burning, nor fear the ghosts that stalk the night.' Smiling, he tugged at one of his coiled gold bracelets till it opened enough for him to slip his wrist out, and tucked it under the baby's hand.

17

Victoria was amazed, but her mother was beaming. 'A royal gift, cousin!'

Arvenic shook his head, tinkling the silver tags on his long braids. 'You're right! King Prasutaeg rewarded me for bravery during the fight, though he didn't support us openly.'

'If he had, and the other tribes had joined us, it's out we'd have driven the cursed Romans!' Cram muttered in his corner. Everybody looked at him. Blushing, he buried his nose in his ale mug.

Arvenic grinned, ruffled his son's hair, and broke the rather awkward silence. 'Young hawk! This one will sing songs of war, not of love!' Shrugging, he smiled at Victoria. 'A fine girl you are, niece, red as a fox your hair and your eyes bright as stars. You have chosen a man?'

'A husband? No!' Victoria exclaimed in disgust. Arvenic laughed. Cram grinned and winked. Cheeky brat! She'd get him! 'You should ask Aegypta, Uncle. She's keen on men. Is Cram, there, looking for a wife?' They both laughed. Good!

Mara was shaking her head. 'A Roman girl can wed at twelve, but usually marries at about eighteen or twenty, cousin. Victoria is only fifteen, she has a few years to go yet.'

'Ah? Three daughters I have about your age, two already wed, and four grandchildren, rolling like puppies round the floor.'

They suddenly realised Rufius was standing in the doorway, listening, his mouth sour in an instant unreasoned dislike. Tired,

18

smelly from inspecting his tannery where hides steeped in old urine and oak bark, muddy from visiting an oyster farm downriver, looking forward to a good wash and a relaxed meal, he was not pleased to find his home full of hairy Celts. Were they angry that their relative had been his slave? Did they want to take her away? Besides, he had to look up to the Celt, which he hated, being short and stocky himself.

There was another babble of introductions and explanations, which Rufius Aegyptus accepted rather grimly while he rinsed his face and slipped on a fresh tunic over the dirty one – the evenings were growing cool. 'Cram is going to be a druid?' His voice was derisive. 'One of the priests who sacrifice men to their gods, and stir up the tribes against us?'

'One man goes willingly every year to gain the favour of the Gods. Romans kill hundreds of gladiators in the arena, for sport! As well as those you slaughter to make peace! Three tribes of Gaul your Caesar wiped out!' Arvenic snorted. 'And for stirring, little is needed, Rufius Aegyptus. Not with your enormous taxes, and seizing our land – it's as well our king was a friend and ally of Rome. What would you demand if he had been an enemy?'

'Cousin, cousin, let that dog sleep!' Mara protested, smiling.

'When is Cram going? The spring?' Rufius hesitated as if to say more but shrugged. 'Well. Good luck to him. But now, I must go out again, there's a town council meeting. Mara, you may of course feed your cousin – I'll deny a meal to no traveller who needs it.' Victoria winced at the implied insult. 'As for what your uncle was saying, he need pity you no longer, Victoria. I've got you a husband. Manlius Drogo.'

She gaped. 'Drogo? The ship captain?'

'He owns two ships. We're going into partnership. Shut your mouth, girl! It's a good match.'

'But – but he's old!' She was almost unable to breathe.

'He is a brute, husband!' Mara cried. 'No decent man will sail with him! You can't give Victoria to an animal like that!'

'A bit rough, yes, but what do looks matter? And he's not old, five years younger than myself. You'll have a house in Burdigala and a couple of slaves, he'll be away most of the time, and he doesn't talk much. What more does any woman want? He'll stop this sword-fighting nonsense – you thought I didn't know? I'm not stupid! But obey and please him when he's home, and you'll do well enough. In any case, you'll do as you're told.'

'No! I won't!' Victoria's temper finally overcame her shock. 'I'd rather die!'

'You disgrace me in public!' Her father slapped her to the ground. 'Then die, girl! A Roman father may slay any of his family who disobey him. Remember that!' He looked ready to hit her again, but glanced aside at the visitors and stamped out.

It was Cram, remembering her sudden fury before, who threw himself forward to intercept Victoria as she snatched up a knife and dived after her father. She knocked Cram spinning, but he had delayed her for just long enough for Arvenic to wrap his arms round her and pick her right off the floor. 'No, niece, no! That will not help!' He held her steadily, easily, while she struggled and cursed.

'Stop, Vicky! Drop that! Behave!' Mara twisted Victoria's hand till the knife fell.

When Victoria eventually stopped kicking, Arvenic set her back on her feet. She shoved him away, gasping dry sobs of fury and humiliation, while he shuffled in embarrassed indignation.

'Outrageous! An old man, a brute – and given no time, no choice and so callously announced, and striking you before strangers – how can any decent man–? Ach! But it is his house, Mara, and your husband he is, I have no right . . .' He tugged at his moustache as if he wanted to rip it off. 'But we'll eat at our wagon. A meal grudged is poison to the soul. Heartily you would guest us, I know, but you will wish to speak alone – and in that man's house – no, I cannot stay here, Mara. To find you, such joy, and then so soon to lose you . . . Any help I can give is yours. Come, Cram—'

'Wait, Father!' The big man stilled at Cram's urgency. 'Aunt, can the smaller children go elsewhere? While we talk?'

Cuddling the howling baby, Mara drew a deep breath, and bent stiffly to Rufinia and Aegyptilla, who were clutching her skirt in distress. 'Now, now, my dears, all over! You know how Vicky sparks up, and how upset Father gets sometimes! Run through to Aegypta in the shop, tell her I said to give you a

21

copper for a sweet cake from the baker, you can share with her. Go on, now.'

Smiling nervously, glad to get away, they scurried out, while Mara sank on to a stool. 'Vicky – oh, Vicky! Drogo has had three wives, everybody knows he killed one by kicking her in the belly while she was pregnant, one died in childbirth, and the last one was killed by thieves because he didn't have decent guards on his house! We can't – I can't – I can't let this happen! Oh, Three Mothers, it's all my fault!'

'Your fault, Mother? Rubbish!' Victoria was biting her knuckles to stop herself cursing. 'It's Father, looking for a profit! Without Drogo's ships, there'd be no question of this wedding. But for them he'll sell his own daughter into slavery. Even a Roman father shouldn't do that!'

'That's why it's my fault.' Mara exchanged a glance with Arvenic. 'I've never told you – when I thought all my family were dead, there seemed to be no reason – and he was so good to us when you were little – but now . . .' She drew a deep breath. 'You're not his daughter.'

'What?' Victoria's knees folded under her, till she was squatting by the table. 'What? He's not – not my father? Truly?' She felt as if lightning had struck her.

'Truth.' Arvenic nodded soberly. 'Your father was Tentoris, my best friend, who was killed during the rebellion. You were captured and sold with your mother, as a baby. You are not even half Roman. You are of the Iceni.'

22

Stunned, trying to take it in, make sense of it, Victoria blinked and swallowed. 'So – yes, I see – I could never please him . . . And *that's* why Father always preferred my sisters! Yes, they look Egyptian, their skin and hair are dark like his, they're not big-boned and red-haired like you and me, Mother.'

Rising from his stool, Cram announced, 'Father, you said we would help. And we can.' As they turned to him, he hesitated, but squared his shoulders and spoke up bravely. 'We must take Boudicca away with us, home to Cheswell.'

They gazed at him, and at each other, in surprise; protested; then, as acceptance grew, began to feel anticipation. Arvenic seemed to grow a hand's breadth in delight at the thought of action against the conquerors. 'You will vanish like the dawn mist, niece – and Mara, too—'

'No. I'll stay.' Mara swallowed, surprisingly calm. 'Don't worry, my dears. Rufius will be angry, of course. He may well beat me, but I'm a free woman now, I can leave if he's too bad. But he won't be, he likes my cooking too much, and he might even be glad to lose Vicky, not that he would ever say so.' She smiled sympathetically at her thunderstruck daughter, and sighed. 'I'll stay here, though. I'm afraid I've gone soft. It's a harder life in the village. You'll see, Vicky. Colder, fewer comforts – and no convenient shops! No, not with a new baby, at the start of winter, after the bad harvest.' She chuckled, rather sourly. 'If he divorces me, you may find me turning up just a few days after you, but it's not likely.'

Mother wasn't too worried, Victoria thought, struggling to accept it all. As well that one of them was calm . . . But Mother had a flexible, comfortable firmness that was seldom long overset. She'd calm her husband. Oh, but there was something else. Victoria had to clear her throat before she could speak. 'But what about Drogo?'

'Oh, Herne the Hunter fly away with him!' Mara chuckled again, more freely. 'There are other owners your father can go into partnership with. But −' she sobered rapidly '− if he discovers where you've gone, Rufius might claim you've been kidnapped and get his legion friends to bring you back, and maybe punish all of our village. They've done it before. They could burn it, take the people as slaves. Your uncle is taking a great risk for you, Vicky.'

Cram nodded round them all. 'Absolutely secret. We must plan very carefully. Sneak you away.'

Uneasily Arvenic tugged his moustache. 'Planning, sneaking, slyness − this is not the way of a warrior.' Cram's face stiffened at the criticism, but his father was shaking his head in grudging admiration. 'Craftier than myself you are, lad, cunning as three foxes! Well fit to be a bard! Anyone would think you were a Roman! But yes, you have the right of it. We must bring no trouble on the tribe.' He huffed again, defiantly. 'But I'll not give my niece up to a brute. You'll be safe with us, girl!'

'Yes − I suppose − yes. Thank you.' Victoria's mind was still whirling. Ten minutes ago, she'd been the eldest daughter of a well-to-do merchant in a growing town. Now, apparently, she was a fugitive, losing her family and friends, her home, everything that was familiar, going to live with savages – no, they weren't savage, whatever Father said, but primitive. What would happen to her? Her heart seemed to be stuck like a wheel between rocks.

She drew deep breaths to get her lungs moving again, and gritted her teeth. She'd not marry Drogo; if that meant she had to live in a ditch and eat worms, she'd do it!

III

Over the next days Victoria escaped from the tension at home, and from her fear of the future, through riding. She must learn before Arvenic came with a horse to rescue her! She had to!

At last, she managed to stick reasonably reliably on the elderly, hammer-headed, rough, leather-mouthed native pony Dio had borrowed for her. 'Told you you could do it, lass!' Dio beamed.

'It's not me!' she objected. 'I just learned to trust the four horns on the saddle. With one sticking up at each corner, there's always something to hold me on.' She still loathed the cursed animal. It didn't matter how hard you dragged on the reins, even with its nose twisted right round to touch its tail it headed off wherever it took a fancy to go, never started or stopped when you wanted it to, twitched and tossed its head, jumped about, twisted and bucked in the middle, bit at one end, dunged at the other, and kicked at both. Who could like it?

At home, as Cram had advised, she kept things looking as ordinary as possible. She worked in the shop, cooked, washed and looked after little Rufinus, to leave Mother free to get on with the preparations for the wedding. To keep up the cover,

Mara ostentatiously packed a chest with Victoria's best tunic and overdress, some sheets and household linens. 'Not that she'll need them, Drogo's house must be well-stocked after three wives!' she snipped at her husband; pretending to be happy about the affair might rouse his suspicions. Aegypta chattered constantly about the wedding, excited and envious. With difficulty, Victoria held in her temper.

With even more difficulty, she was polite to her father. Rufius was defiantly Roman, refusing to wear the native trousers that sensible men wore under their tunics, even while he shivered in the cool mornings. He was determined to go ahead with the wedding, but kinder than usual, almost conciliatory, as if underneath, he was ashamed of what he was doing – not that he'd ever admit it, of course. He brought in a length of rich fabric, the finest wool Mara had ever seen, crimson for good fortune. 'For her bridal dress, wife. The priest at Claudius the God's temple says the fourth day from now will be a lucky day.' He hesitated, and made quite a concession. 'Will Arvenic still be in Londinium? He may wish to attend.'

'No, husband, they left two days ago.' He nodded, well-satisfied.

Victoria kept her eyes on the barley flour she was grinding, and clamped down on the fury that still roiled whenever she saw him. And the panic. Savages, the Iceni were, they worshipped snakes . . . No. Mother said not. But would they tattoo her? Mother had a tattoo on her shoulder and neck, spikes and swirls to signal her family and tribe, as a blessing and protection.

The person most upset was, oddly enough, old Bron. His doggy face fell into even more mournful folds. He muttered, where Rufius could hear him, 'That Drogo, he beat two men to death last year, he's killed three wives, it's not right!' and narrowly missed being whipped for his trouble. His doleful eyes followed Victoria about whenever he was in the house, till she felt like hitting him.

And then, the very day before the marriage, when she was almost ready to run away alone, a boy stopped her in the street. 'Hey, Victoria? A tall Iceni man said to tell you he'll meet you after sunset just beyond the new wool warehouse. Bit old for you, though!' He winked as she snarled at him playfully, and trotted off whistling the latest love song.

At last!

Then she saw Bron, not four arm-lengths away, looking alarmed.

She grabbed his tunic. 'You heard that? You tell Father and I'll murder you!'

He just stood and looked at her, silently, until she felt silly. He had always been good to her . . . 'Sorry. You won't, will you?' He walked off without a word. He wouldn't. Would he?

That evening they went to bed, as normal, at sunset. The girls had been scurrying about since dawn, as usual, but tonight

28

for some reason they seemed to take ages to fall asleep. Finally, though, Victoria could slip from the big bed. Would she ever see them again? She nearly risked kissing them farewell, but they might wake. In her parents' bed at the other end of the attic, Father was snoring gently. Bron hadn't told him, thanks to the Triple Goddess that Mother always swore by!

Mara, lying wakeful and tense, slid from under the quilt, and they crept down the ladder to the kitchen. They couldn't risk candle-light disturbing anyone; Mara blew to waken the charcoal stove, and in its dim glow Victoria dressed warmly. 'I've put food and clothes in your pack, Vicky, and coral earrings, a gift for your Aunt Aliss.' They glided through the store, eased the front door open–

A shadow rose from behind the counter. Victoria's knife was in her hand instantly.

Bron almost squawked in alarm. 'No, no, young mistress – I'm not – I'll help you!'

She eyed him suspiciously. 'Why?'

'Sh! I can't—' Bron swallowed, and started again. 'I've served the master now for seventeen years. Longer than you've been alive! There's far worse, but you and your mother, you treat me like one of the family. And it's not right, marrying you to that— And you can't go wandering about at night alone, not among the drunks and roughs, no, not even you, young mistress, it's not safe. So I'll go with you.' Valiantly the old man hefted the cudgel they kept under the counter.

Victoria snorted. 'What good d'you think you can—' Then she stopped. The old man risked her father flogging him, maybe having him crucified, for helping her escape; he dared to go out in the dark to guard her from attack, when he was terrified himself. 'Bron, you're heroic.'

'Oh, no – but a man there might help keep off robbers and drunks. And I – er – I got you this.' From his bed under the counter he produced something the length of his forearm, thin and heavy.

A sword. Small, shorter and lighter than modern army ones, gleaming darkly in the moonlight. She rubbed her fingers down the smooth, shining coldness, in love already. 'It's razor-sharp! Oh, thank you! I'm a real warrior maiden now!'

Mara eyed the sword doubtfully while Victoria sheathed it again and belted the scabbard on her right hip. 'Where did you get that, Bron?' she whispered. 'You didn't steal it?'

'No, no, mistress! It's from Hispania, I bought it from a packman.'

'With your savings?' Most slaves drank or gambled away any coins they gained, but she knew Bron had been saving hard, hoping eventually to buy himself free. For him to give up his own dreams, to help Victoria . . . 'Oh, Bron!' Mara kissed his pouchy cheek.

'Oh, no, mistress!' Bashfully, he hobbled out into the lane.

'Mother . . . I can't leave you!'

Mara tried to smile. 'Don't be silly. And don't make a tragedy out of it, my dear! Think of it as a great adventure – isn't that what you've always wanted? We'll be all right. No, dear, you must go now. The Triple Goddess guard you till we meet again, my darling!' Trying not to sob aloud, Mara stood by the door to watch her daughter sneak off round the corner.

As it happened, Victoria and Bron didn't see a soul in the black streets. Just beyond the last buildings, where the ancient pathway of Ermine Street, being rebuilt by the army, led out north among the farmlands, a man appeared from a copse of pollarded willow trees. Bron gasped and lifted the cudgel, but Victoria gripped his wrist. 'Arvenic?'

'Boudicca? Who's that?'

'A friend,' she whispered. 'A good friend, Uncle. Better than I knew.'

She could almost feel Bron blush beside her, but he shook his head. 'No, no . . . If the master finds out – oh, well . . .' In the moonlight, his face was blue. He took her hands. 'I'll raise the alarm at dawn, say I heard you creeping out, thought you were going to the shrine to pray, followed you to make sure you were safe, and you went down to the wharf and threw yourself in the river. So I'll shout there, call for help, I couldn't jump in after you, I can't swim. If your body's never found, well, the river's deep. And then master won't seek for you.'

She hugged him, the last person of her old life. 'Bron, you're worth your weight in silver. I'm sorry about all

31

the times I teased you! Take care of yourself, and Mother, and the girls. And little Rufinus. And – yes, and Father too, I suppose.'

'Don't cry, now! The Gods go with you, child.'

Glad to have something to distract her, Victoria clambered on to one of the ponies that Arvenic led out from the trees. It twitched. She slipped off. Bron helped her climb back on. She gathered up the reins, and wobbled as the animal shied. 'Stupid beast, that was only an owl!'

'You told me you could ride!' Arvenic complained, shoving her upright again.

'On a proper saddle, not just a tied-on sheepskin!' she snarled. He snorted, swung a long leg over his own pony, nearly reaching the ground on either side, and started away.

Victoria clutched the mane wildly as her pony jumped to follow. 'Goodbye, Bron!' and muttered curses floated back.

Bron waved, knowing she was not watching. Jupiter, let the master believe him!

In one way, the riding was good for Victoria. She was too busy to fret, regret, worry, weep. The spirited young animal, far livelier than Dio's elderly slug, knew its rider was a novice. It raced its team-mate, or stopped suddenly and jerked its head down to snatch a mouthful of grass. Arvenic was no help; he laughed every time she fell off. 'We Iceni are horse-folk. You must learn to master your mount!'

Her temper rose, and with it a bitter determination. She'd show him!

'Aren't you scared of ghosts, Uncle?' she demanded. 'Mother gave me a charm to protect me.' She touched the little carved hazelnut at her throat.

He chuckled. 'When night falls and demons can walk, most folk shut themselves up safe, but my own charm I have. In my head.'

'A prayer?'

'A piece from a Roman sword, that broke off in my skull. With that iron in my head, what spirit will come near me?' His teeth gleamed in the moonlight. 'So we are both safe, Boudicca. Even if people wake to hear us passing, they'll believe us ghosts. Safe we may travel, and unseen save by deer and wolves, boar or bear, or the wild white cattle, or the Little People of the hills who see but are not seen.'

Wolves? And bears? And the Little People? Oh, well. Better than Drogo.

At dawn they stopped well off the road, avoiding farmers or hunters who might gossip about them. Moving stiffly, Victoria got cold meat and bread out of her pack, while Arvenic hobbled the ponies to graze. She ate standing wide-legged, lay down carefully under a tree out of the worst of the wet, and was asleep in three breaths.

When she woke that afternoon, her thighs and calves were raw, her unpractised, over-strained muscles were agony, her legs ached from dangling unsupported for so long. She gritted her teeth to stop herself moaning. To her relief Arvenic didn't comment at her winces when she climbed back on her pony. However, when they passed an outlying Roman farm, he left her for a while and reappeared with a sheep. That dawn they ate sumptuously, the grease soothed her blisters, and the extra padding of the fleece under her from then on was wonderful.

For two more nights they rode cross-country. 'I sent the wagons up the straight road through Camulodunum, but due north we'll head, towards the Catuvellaun hills further away than our lands, and then cut back south-east, through the marshes. We must avoid sentry-posts and questions.'

'Lots of soldiers there, aren't there? I know Camulodunum is a colony of veterans whose legion disbanded there. It's supposed to keep the tribes quiet.'

'Paid off they were with Trinovantes' land that they seized, and drove off or enslaved the true owners!' Arvenic grumbled. 'Our turn next, unless the gods favour us.'

She nodded. 'They don't know me, of course, but they'd recall us if Father inquires later.'

'Best to take no chances,' the Iceni agreed. 'But soon home we will be in Cheswell, niece.'

Home. Home was Londinium, Mother, family . . . No, not any longer.

Gradually the pain diminished. In the afternoons, before

they started out, Victoria did her exercises. At least it worked off the stiffness. To her surprise, her new sword wasn't much heavier than Dio's wooden practice one, and it was better balanced. Arvenic laughed at her. 'What a dainty little pin!'

She turned the laughter back at him. 'That's what I'll call it – Pin!'

'She. A sword is like a ship or a spear, always a woman. My own sword is Ice Witch. And remember, draw blood you must always, whenever your sword sees light.'

She blinked. She had never heard this one. 'You're not joking?'

'Certainly not. A sacrifice to the spirit of the blade, that she will not turn against you in spite.'

'I'll remember that.' She poked her arm, carefully, till a drop of blood gleamed bright on the bronze. 'Pin, I love you! And your pinprick is dangerous!' She thrust at his belly, as Dio had taught her, so that he had to jump back, and grinned in a bawdy triumph.

'Ach!' Arvenic grunted disgust. 'Ice Witch is twice as long. Three halves you would be in before you got near enough to poke holes in me!'

'I thought the Romans disarmed the tribes, that was what started your revolt.'

He winked. 'Aye, years ago. Let them search now, in the thatch and round the barns, and it's surprised they'd be, niece!

But if you could get inside the swing and stab – yes, maybe you could do damage.'

'It's how the legions fight, and they beat you.' She stuck her tongue out at him.

'Last time. Not next time.' He was suddenly so grim, her smile faded. But he grinned again. 'Certainly not if Cram has his way. That boy – fiercer than a wildcat against the Romans!'

On the third night they turned east off Ermine Street, down off the hills, and rode for a day and a half among woodland and marshes. No wide paved road slashed through the bogs here, only occasional muddy tracks. They twisted to and fro through alder and willow scrubland and forest, forded across and across meandering, shallow streams, and occasionally swam deeper ones; splashed round black pools where mad-eyed herons stalked eels, leeches and frogs among the tall whispering reeds. 'We're right out on the north edge of Iceni land. Even the King's men can scarcely find us!' Arvenic boasted.

Why would they want to, Victoria wondered, irritably scratching midge bites.

At last, in the grey of a wet evening, the track rose, the trees fell back on to open moorland. A few herd-boys waved to them, leading herds of ponies, small black cattle, goats and little brownish sheep among a scattered patchwork of narrow fields, up a slight rise towards a wooden wall. She gulped at the old skulls on the posts; that was what happened to enemy heads, was it? Above the palisade, smoke rose from the thatched peaks of a score of round huts. 'Cheswell!' Arvenic declared proudly. 'Small, compared to the king's town at Venta, but the stockade is strong against Catuvellaun raiders – or Romans!'

The grey light just matched Victoria's mood of apprehension and anxiety.

At the blast of the watchman's horn, it all changed. Two hundred people came charging out, ignoring the drizzle. She hung on grimly till her pony quietened enough for her to slip off as if she meant to, and her sour spirits began to lift. The noise refreshed her – cheers, shouting, ululating cries from the women, dogs barking and children yelling. Bright colours, checks and stripes glowed cheerfully in the last light. Everyone looked happy. It might not be so bad.

Above her, Arvenic raised his arms for silence. 'Welcome Mara's daughter, Boudicca, returned from the grave – or from Londinium, which is worse!'

Amid the cheering, a small, wiry woman in a flurry of red fringes pulled Victoria's head down to kiss her cheek. 'I am Aliss, mistress of the fire in this house, Boudicca. Be welcome!' As her husband swept her up into his arms to kiss her, she scolded him, 'Put me down, you great bear! What will our guest think of you?'

'That I'm a barbarian – but that she knows already!' Everyone joined in the laughter.

'Poor girl, falling off your feet with tiredness you are, and freezing cold and damp – if you've not taken a fever it will be a surprise. Come in, my dear, warm yourself, eat, rest. Arvenic, Cram has been bizzing about like a bee at a buttercup, waiting to speak with you urgently!' She rolled her eyes in comic exaggeration. 'But he won't say why.'

'Is he worried about me?' Victoria asked. 'I know it's a danger for you, Mother told me—'

'No, no!' Aliss reassured her. 'Some rumour he picked up. Oh, there's himself now.' She beamed at her son as he crutched through the crowd. 'You smelt your supper? Here's your father at last, then. What's bothering at you?'

'Greetings, cousin, I'm glad you are safe.' Cram smiled briefly at Victoria. 'Father, may I speak to you alone? Though everyone will need to know soon, I suppose.'

Arvenic studied his son for a second, and then turned to the clustering crowd, shooing them all away. 'Is our guest a dancing bear, so? Is there no work to do at all?'

They moved away good-naturedly, while Aliss beckoned her family and Victoria into the hut. Cram glanced round to check that no-one was listening, and murmured, 'Father, while we passed through Camulodunum – a secret it's supposed to be, but all the slaves know. The cursed Romans ignore them, think of them as furniture, but they listen, they know more Latin than they admit to.'

'Well? What did they tell you?'

'The tribes in Wales are still fighting, and the Romans know the druids encourage them, as they helped Caractacus before.

So in the spring, as soon as the grass grows enough to feed horses on the move, General Suetonius plans to take two legions, the Twentieth Valeria from Camulodunum and the Fourteenth Gemina from Viroconium, and attack Mona. They plan to kill the druids. All of them.'

IV

In her first few days, Victoria offended almost everyone in the village. She couldn't help it; when she saw something being done differently from the Roman way – baking, or training a dog, or sharpening a knife – she couldn't help saying so. As she saw it, it was one way of not being so helpless, so much an outsider, a stranger; but they were insulted, and showed it.

'Stop instructing people,' Aliss advised. 'You seem to be showing off, acting arrogant or superior.' Victoria apologised, and did her best to hold her tongue in future, but the damage had been done.

Her family and some of the village folk made allowances for her different upbringing, realised she was trying to help, and occasionally even accepted her new ideas.

Others didn't. The young people of her own age, even Arvenic's daughters who should have been her friends, were cold and unfriendly, led by a handsome, arrogant young man named Mac Clanna.

The first time they met, the evening of her arrival, he flashed his big blue eyes and charming smile at her. He and his entourage of three girls and four young men clearly expected her to fall under his glamour and kiss his feet in admiration.

When she did not – he reminded her somehow of Myron, in Londinium – he took an instant, insulted dislike to her, as Rufius had done to Arvenic, and never let a meeting pass without a sneer of some kind.

Her temper grew edgy. Then edgier.

Out in the woods one day she heard a slapping noise, and whimpering, and found Mac Clanna slapping a skinny slave boy's face, over and over – and grinning, as if he enjoyed it. The lad's head dangled, rocking with the blows. She tutted in disgust at the bullying.

'Stupid, careless, handless brat!' Mac Clanna snarled at her. Then, as his eyes focused and he became aware of her, his whole attitude changed. He dropped the boy and stepped carelessly over him, turning his full attention on to Victoria. He strutted forward, preening, snaking his head up and back, flexing his smooth muscles, half-smiling, licking his lips, eyeing her up and down with his eyes half closed, humming appreciatively. He took her hand, gazing deep into her eyes . . .

Victoria started to giggle.

She couldn't help it; he thought he was so wonderful, so overwhelming, but only a month before, she had seen Certinus doing exactly the same thing with the barmaid from next door in Londinium, and so much better! And with appreciation and liking, not contempt. Did he really think she would just ignore how he had been treating the lad lying at their feet? He must be crazy!

Of all the things she could have done to hurt Mac Clanna, laughing at him when he was in full display was the worst. He stopped dead, his jaw dropping, turned red and then pale with fury. He raised a hand to hit her, but thought better of it when she stiffened, ready to defend herself. She stood and stared at him, not fully realising how much she had offended him, trying to stifle the giggles that escaped in little snorts and spurts, like bubbles from a bottle, till he spun round and stalked off.

'Oh, dear me! Conceited nitwit! Even Aegypta would have laughed at him!' Still fizzing with glee, she turned to see to the boy left snivelling on the bracken.

Slaves, of course, did the heaviest, dirtiest work, and got the poorest food and clothing. Some were prisoners taken in raids. Old or weak-spirited people sometimes sold themselves, to be sure of food and shelter, however meagre. Starving parents might sell a child to buy food for the rest of the family. Others were sentenced to slavery for debt, or middling-serious crimes like laming a dog, or moving a border stone; worse than killing someone, for which they would be fined, and not as bad as harming a horse, which would mean death. But no sensible person deliberately ill-treated slaves; as the luck turned, you might be a slave yourself next year.

'Ach, look at your nose, it's bleeding like a fountain!' She helped the lad to sit up. 'Come along to Aliss, we'll wash your face, and Arvenic will speak to Mac Clanna about it, tell him to treat you reasonably.'

The boy clung to her hand. 'No, please! It was my fault – I dropped his arrows and trod on one and broke it – please, please, if you say anything, he'll just be worse. Please, just leave it, please!' He gazed at her beseechingly. 'And please, miss, don't tell anybody about – about laughing at him. Or he'll kill me!'

He was so frantic that, though he must be exaggerating, to his vast relief she agreed to keep it quiet. In Londinium a slave might well have been flogged for damaging arrows. A beating, even so nasty, was not too bad, after all. Besides, it was not really her business – and when the boy himself wanted her to do nothing . . . She shrugged and let the lad scamper off home.

For some days the memory of Mac Clanna's frustration amused her. Occasionally she saw the little boy creeping nervously about, his face bruised and swollen, but after a few days he disappeared. When she asked, Aliss said, 'He's run away. No loss – a stupid, clumsy lad, always in trouble. Nobody will bother to chase him to fetch him back!'

It wasn't till the next day that a horrible suspicion came to Victoria; had the boy run off? Or had Mac Clanna done what the lad had feared?

No. That was silly. She thrust the thought firmly away. There was no proof of anything, and nobody would be that evil.

Things were bad enough for herself. She began to hear behind her every day, almost every hour, murmured taunts from Mac Clanna and his friends. 'Know-all!' 'Can't skin a deer.' 'Have you seen her on a horse?' 'Can't understand a word she says, in that accent.' 'Thinks she's the biggest apple!' And worst of all, 'Roman spy!' But nothing to her face. Her amusement faded rapidly, to frustration and anger.

Living in a room with no corners didn't help; it was unnatural, made her feel uneasy. The big, dim hut was colder than she was used to, even crouching on the stools and chests that circled the central fire-pit. The heat rose with the smoke to hang in a haze four feet up, drying and preserving the winter's store already started, the split salmon dangling up under the steep, high roof among knots of eels, rings of trout strung on willow withies, strings of oysters, mushrooms and onions, bunches of herbs, before filtering out through the reed thatch. Hides slung between the rafters held sacks and bundles.

Three looms where the women wove bright-chequered cloth made an open partition on one side between the tree-trunk pillars that supported the centres of the rafters. The thane and his wife and family, and also Victoria, as a guest, slept there, cosy beside the fire amid – and often under – a horde of dogs of assorted sizes and colours, from rat-killing terriers to the huge shaggy hounds that were a valuable export to Rome, to fight in the arena there. Four young men from another village, here to train as warriors, slept on the other side of the fire, and the house slaves in the outer, coldest part, by the low mud-plastered walls.

One afternoon Victoria came into the hut, and found it unexpectedly deserted. No children, no women working on the looms – but a young man kneeling in her sleeping place. 'Who's that? Oh, it's you, Mac Clanna.' She hesitated, but clenched her teeth and smiled. If she showed she was ready to forgive and forget, be friendly, maybe he would do the same?

Then she saw what he was holding. 'Dog dirt? To rub in my furs? You pig-turd!'

'Is that stink not natural for a Roman bitch?' he gibed.

Some of his friends appeared in the doorway to support him, guffawing.

Victoria was too angry to notice, or care. She seized the shuttle from a loom, and erupted.

They jeered, and snatched to disarm her; then stopped laughing as the wood cracked heads and wrists. Shocked, they began to fight back. But they got in each other's way, while she knew that anyone she hit was an enemy. A loom crashed down. A swung stool half-stunned her. She went berserk, lashing out wildly, screeching, far beyond reason. Her hand knocked against the hilt of her sword, forgotten till then, and she snatched it out with a scream of triumph. They jumped back. Someone drew a knife.

45

Suddenly, Cram was there. He didn't waste time exclaiming or arguing, but picked up the cauldron of water by the fire and upended it over Victoria's head. 'Stop! Stand, all of you!'

Choking, blinded, the girl fought the pot off her head. By then she was sobered enough to recognise Cram, and stand still, wiping her face, blinking in surprise as he berated his friends.

'Four of you, against one girl, and she a guest!' His voice was somehow deeper than normal. 'The guest is sacred. That is the strongest geas of all, the oldest commandment of the gods, the most sacred rule, the deepest curse, set upon every soul. Undying shame to break it it is! Your parents' faces are blackened by the dishonour of their children. What does this act show about you – that you are clever, or brave, or noble? I'll make a song about you that will be sung for years – the shameless brats who tried to embarrass a guest, beaten by a girl with a stick.' In Londinium, everyone would have laughed at the lad, so pompous; but these louts stood abashed. Suddenly the impressive voice broke; 'Oh, clear out before my father comes in. Or my mother – it's skin you alive she would!'

They slunk out fast, nursing bruises, Mac Clanna holding his swollen mouth where he had lost a tooth. Victoria grinned after them, pleased by their discomfiture despite her sore head. 'How do you do that? Make your voice boom? A bard's trick?'

She expected him to wink and explain, but he was too

46

annoyed. 'Never mind that. Help me pick up the loom. Ach, see Mother's good weaving, all muddy and trampled and the bobbins tangled! Boudicca, that was shameful!'

'I couldn't let him get away with it!' she protested.

'Who would ask you to?' To her astonishment, Cram agreed with her. What irked him was that she had not been fighting well. 'You weren't thinking! Father says if people think they can beat you, they're more likely to fight. If your sword you had drawn, they'd have run out, no-one would have been hurt, and Mother's weaving would still be clean. You must think! They might have disgraced us even worse by hurting you. You're not Cuchulain, who grew to ten times mortal size in battle!'

'Checky imp!' She clattered his sticking-out ears for him.

'Get off me, you giantess!' He batted her hand away, but finally relaxed and chuckled. 'Ach, at least you didn't kill anybody and start a blood feud. But watch out, Mac Clanna loathes being beaten, and it's a bitter memory he has.'

She stopped, suddenly sober, and while she put on a dry shirt told him her suspicions about the slave boy. What should she do?

Mopping up the water with her damp tunic, Cram puffed thoughtfully. 'I think you are wrong, Boudicca. Even if you are not, without proof you can do nothing. You must leave it. Remember it, keep your eye open for any actual evidence, but until then, nothing. Stop and think before you act.'

Victoria sighed. 'I suppose you're right. Dio said much the same thing. I must learn to control my temper, or I'll never fight really well.'

His face stiffened as it always did when she mentioned Romans in less than a critical way. Ach, well; it was just the way he was. She picked up the cauldron and went out to refill it.

Autumn was the busiest time of year for the village. The grains and beans were threshed and stored in bins. 'The third poor harvest in a row,' Aliss grumbled. 'We'll need to buy in grain next summer, I'm afraid.' Pears and apples, plums, medlars and brambles were dried, pickled or racked. The bee-skeps were smoked out and the honey and wax stored. Hay to feed the animals over the winter was used to blanket storage pits of parsnips and cabbage against snow and frost, and much of the winter's supply of firewood was dragged home and piled handy by hut doors.

Now that the grass was dying, all the beasts not needed for breeding next year had to be slaughtered. The fat was melted down into hide sacks to make candles later, the meat salted, spiced and hung in the smoke; sheets of beef and horse-meat, legs and sides of mutton and pork, tangles of sausages. Everybody, even the slaves, stuffed themselves greasy, fattening for the winter. The dogs were in ecstasy. The hides were scraped, salted and rolled, to be cured properly when they had time. They used every scrap of a pig, Aliss chuckled, except the squeal.

To leave Aliss and the slaves free for butcher-work, Victoria helped with the daily tasks. The everlasting spinning and weaving were abandoned for the moment, and the slaves saw to the animals, but she cooked stews and roasts, and baked flat scones on a pan, and small loaves under an upturned pot with ashes piled over it, as Mother did at home.

No; in Londinium . . .

She had heard nothing from her family in Londinium, which in one way relieved her – Mother must be all right, surely? – and sometimes worried her – maybe Mother was dead?

She made a little private sacrifice to the Three Mothers, to keep her own mother safe and well.

Cram was delighted to teach her the prayers and small sacrifices to be offered when you drew water or cut wood or went hunting or helped birth a calf or a foal. 'Everything has its spirit, trees and wells and animals. If you offend it, the well may dry up, or the animals die or move away so you go hungry.'

To her relief, though, Mother was right; the Iceni didn't worship snakes. Their only contact with serpents was an old, withered widow who kept some adders in a pit by the gate. She said that by how they acted, she could foretell the future, predict the weather, or find lost objects. Once she had found a lost child. Victoria did wonder whether it could be plain common sense that made her tell them to seek the adventurous toddler in the dark, scary nemet, the grove of trees sacred to the gods. He was found, though, before wolves or bears got him, so she kept her doubts to herself.

Mara had told Victoria about the tribal priests, the druids, who spent long years in study, to develop their powers and skills, as teachers, warriors, bards, physicians. They were called in as impartial judges in disputes between chieftains, or to settle blood feuds.

Father said the priest druids sacrificed captured Roman soldiers.

Of course they sacrificed to the gods; something valuable or hard to get, for what gods would favour people who gave them worthless gifts? But nothing appalling. Usually. Ale to the sea-god Manannan – everyone knew what sailors liked; a wren to Rhiannon of the birds; songs and honey cakes to Ceridwen, goddess of inspiration; the king stallion to Lugh, the sun-god, at the early autumn feast of Lughnasadh once in three years; and a mare every year at Beltane to the Iceni's great goddess, Epona of the horses. Only on Mona, nowadays, was a human offering chosen, usually a red-haired man. At times of war, though, they did darker magic.

Like now . . .

Arvenic normally officiated at sacrifices, as the village was too small and isolated to have its own druid. However, this year one walked out of the forest on the day before the full moon at the end of October, as the Romans called it. 'I am Con Veile, ovate of the Third Level. I have come to conduct Samhain, the

Feast of the Dead.' She was cheerful, middle-aged, unexpectedly motherly in her black robe. But what had Victoria expected? A skinny, bearded ancient with blood under his nails?

'The ovates are the druids who can speak to the dead, and read the future,' Cram whispered. 'In the stars and clouds, or the flight of birds – or the blood and guts of a sacrifice.'

'Reliably?' Victoria murmured, and blushed as she saw the druid watching them.

Aliss herself served mead, to honour the visitor, while Cram told his news about Mona. Con Veile smiled at him. 'We hear their plans, never fear! But well done, that you discovered the scheme, and even more that you kept quiet, rather than shouting about it and warning the Romans that we knew. We will be ready for them.'

Just before sunset, the close of the day as of the year, Con Veile faced the whole village in the open centre of the nemet, beside the pillar-stone that was the heart of their land. On it she had laid a bunch of herbs and her sacred knife, a flint blade long and slender as a finger, delicate as a butterfly's wing, sharp as any iron point, tied with a thong of human skin into a sturdy hazel haft. As a future bard, Cram was acting as her assistant. He proudly held her silver cup and a green glass jar of magic mistletoe ointment.

Arvenic and the men stood to her left; Aliss led Victoria and the women to her right, all wearing their finest, bearing lit torches in the slanting light below the branches. Nearby was

51

piled wood and the greasy rubbish and bones from the butchering.

Con Veile raised her oak staff, its head hung with little golden bells which she rang to draw silence. 'You have heard, the Romans mean to attack the island of Mona in the spring.' A growl of anger rose from the throng. 'You want to help us drive back the Romans?' They shouted agreement, waving their torches, but her voice rose above their clamour. 'You must not!'

In the sudden hush, she spoke stern as rock. 'We druids can and will defend our sacred island. But if you fight alongside us, they will know, and will come against you in power to take revenge. We cannot prevent that, not now. Not yet. Soon the tribes will join together to drive them out. Soon, soon – it has been foreseen!' She raised a hand to calm them. 'But not now. Not now! For now, you must trust us to defend Mona. Stay clear, stay here!'

The older people nodded, remembering the devastation after the rising against the Romans a dozen years before. The young men glowered. True, there was a school of warriors on Mona, famed for producing the fiercest fighting men and women in Britain. Against that and the druids' powers the Romans could scarcely hope for success. But still . . .

'Sorrow, sorrow to lose the chance of a fight! But we hear your words, lady,' Arvenic called, voicing their disappointment. 'We will stand aside for now.' He grinned round. 'But we'll lift

52

the swords from the thatch, and sharpen them ready. We have eaten too much submission, lolled in idleness too long!' Victoria joined in the cheering.

The druid raised her arms towards the last of the sunlight striking level under the twisted, ancient branches. The bells on her staff tinkled gently as she chanted.

'The year ends, and begins; turns, and returns!

Summer sinking, cold creeping.

Wind whistling; sun sunken, short-shining.

Stags belling, roaring their challenge in the silence of snow.

Wild geese flying, fleeting from afar.

Trees frilled with frost, leaves lying, bracken blood-brown, broken;

Earth and water icy, stilled in this sleeping season.

Store-rooms stocked with Cernunnos' bounty.

Crisp crunching of footsteps,

Flashing flames fire the dark,

Homely, happy hearth,

Fine feasting, singing and storytelling,

Warm welcome for wayfarers.

People, be patient; endure, enjoy; summer will be reborn!'

She turned to the waiting crowd. 'Honour we now the third form of the Triple Goddess of Life, of creation and destruction, love and hatred, life and death. Her youngest form, Bridhe, the innocent Maiden, brings us the hope that renews our youth each spring. Macha, generous summer

Mother of love and fertility, nourishes, warms and comforts us. But the Cailleach, the Old Woman, offers the bitter courage to endure the winter, and cold wisdom to guide us through our life to the gates of death. All reverence and respect, fear and worship to her today.

'Cailleach, old woman, do not strike the ground too hard with your ice hammer! Veiled one, accept our sacrifice. Wise one, let the frosts not be too fierce and long, to freeze our children – but not too soft either, to weaken us. Bring us strong to a new spring. Cold one, grant a peaceful passage to the Land of Youth to those whose lives are done, but with your black hammer bring doom to our enemies!'

The old snake woman led forward a sow garlanded with leaves and berries. It had been fed poppy seed and aconite to make it drowsy and easy to control. However, when the druid anointed its forehead, pressing to make it nod acceptance of its fate, it suddenly panicked. Since men could not touch the Goddess's anointed animal, Victoria and Aliss leapt to help the old woman trip it and hold it as it kicked and squealed.

Con Veile had to shout above the din, chanting words they could not understand as she stabbed down with the flint knife.

As the sow struggled, she missed a swift kill. Its blood fountained, splattering the druid's robe. Screaming in frenzy, biting and kicking, the beast knocked the druid to her knees. The silver cup she held to catch its blood was jolted from her hand, and a hound, a black dog, the colour of death, slunk out of the crowd, and licked the blood in the sacrificial cup. The worst of all omens.

Someone speared it, but too late. A moan of dismay ran round the audience. 'Evil! We are accursed!' Some hid their faces in fear. One woman had hysterics.

Mac Clanna shouted, 'It's that Roman girl! The gods are offended!' Though he was hushed, several people glared at Victoria, wondering . . .

Victoria's temper flared at the accusation. It wasn't her fault! But nobody was moving. They all stood frozen by their religious awe. Somebody had to do something. She'd show them she wasn't scared to move! She stepped forward and picked up the cup. Someone hissed, but the druid didn't object. That gave her permission. She ran to wash the cup at the well, careful not to let the polluted water fall back in and anger the spirit of the pool.

'Well done, my dear!' Aliss whispered, white-faced, when she brought it back.

Collecting fresh blood, the druid announced, 'The sacrifice is accepted.' She held her face serene, but her voice was strained.

Quickly, the women cut up the sow and laid the god's share on the wood pile. The old woman set the head respectfully on the heart stone. Into a cauldron of water Con Veile mixed the blood and some of her ointment, and stirred it with the leaves Cram held. 'From Mona, mistletoe, sage and juniper, holly and ivy, blessed by the High Druid.' She sprinkled the heart stone,

55

and the sow's head, and walked round the circle sprinkling all the trees. 'Cailleach, Triple Goddess, accept our offering, guard and guide us, grant us your hope, your courage, your love, your wisdom, your fortitude. All gods, join with us, give us your blessing.'

Aliss came forward with her torch. In the gathering dark, Con Veile scooped some of the mixture from the cauldron in the little cup for her to drink, and sprinkled her forehead. 'Cailleach, bless us!' Aliss called, and thrust her torch below the pile of wood. Arvenic followed her. In turn, man and woman, everyone came forward to be hallowed, and add their torches to the blaze. Victoria's heart twisted at the bitter taste, the cold spatter of holy liquid on her face. The flames leapt up, spluttering and gulping at the greasy bones heaped above the wood, spiralling and swirling up greedily, tossing sparks high into the dark sky. The pig was spitted and set to roast, though with little of the normal rejoicing, while an old man Victoria had only ever noticed snoozing in warm corners, a retired bard, recited all Arvenic's ancestors for sixty generations.

Sipping a cup of ale, Arvenic grimaced. 'The bone-fire burns well, at least! It's no more bad omens we're needing! Con Veile – the beast acting like that, and then the dog. I don't believe it was Boudicca being here, there has been no sign of any disfavour from the gods before, but – druid, what caused it? What does it mean?'

'Disaster. Death. Maybe for the Romans.' The druid was grim. 'I must consult with the High Druid . . .' She shivered where she stood by the roaring fire. 'Store plenty of food for yourselves and for your beasts. A cold time is coming.'

'What do you see, lady?' Cram dared to whisper. This was the turn of the year, when the gates of the otherworld opened briefly between the worlds of living and dead. This one night the spirits of their ancestors could re-cross the bridge of swords to walk the land again until cock-crow, and speak through flame or darkness, blood and omens to those sensitive to them.

The druid's face and hands were crimsoned by the roaring fire, and smeared blood. Clutching her golden-belled branch, she stared blankly into the flames. 'The ravens and wolves will feed well . . .' She started, and came to herself. 'You were going to Mona this spring, Cram? No. Stay by your father.' She gestured to stop his protest. 'No. When the fighting is over, you will be welcome, if—'

'If what?'

'If ?' Again her mind had to return from afar. 'Ah. If you still wish to come. For now, play your harp, make songs, learn what you can from your old bard.' She waved him away.

'That wasn't what that she was going to say,' he muttered to Victoria.

'Mm. I think she meant, if they drive the Romans back from Mona.'

He glared at her. 'They? You mean we?'

'Yes, of course!' But he had turned away from her. He limped over to where Mac Clanna and his friends were strutting and posing to draw attention.

She huffed angrily, but he had a point. Whose side *was* she on, deep down? It should be the Iceni, shouldn't it? But did she want her friends in Londinium killed? Life was difficult.

If . . . ? If the druids won? She felt her hair prickle.

Con Veile was staring at her. Uneasy at the intense gaze, Victoria turned aside.

The druid murmured, 'Your niece, that tall, sturdy girl with fox-red hair?'

Aliss smiled. 'Reared as a Roman, but Iceni by blood and heart. We think to have her tattooed this winter, and adopt her at Beltane.'

'No.' The druid sighed. 'That is not her fate. Arvenic, the gods tell me to lay this geas on you and your kin. Guard your niece, Boudicca. Guard her well. She is important to you. To all of us.'

Arvenic in his turn stared at her. 'Important? For good or ill, lady? Guard her? Is it guard ourselves from her that you mean, or guard her from her enemies?'

The druid shook her head, bothered by her visions. 'Oh, she wishes you no harm. But she may bring it on you. Or she may do you great good . . . Keep her safe, I mean. You will need her, in the end. Or your son will.'

'Cram?' Arvenic frowned. 'What can she do for him?'

'If I knew, I would tell you. The flames show only what the gods wish, not what I would see.' Shivering, she let Aliss lead her indoors and lend her a clean gown. But at the feast, when traditionally everyone ate and drank to bursting point, she ate little, and sat silent instead of joining the dancing lines circling the oak trees.

V

The cold, short days of winter were a time of rest – or perhaps just of work more indoors than out. The women had the normal housework, the spinning, weaving, sewing and cooking. 'A blind bear could do better!' Aliss exclaimed in disgust at Victoria's sewing, and herself made her niece a green-and-red checked tunic and breeches, like a boy's.

Cram already knew most of the old bard's songs, and practised with his harp Larksong till at last when he took her from her embroidered bag people stopped groaning, and listened with pleasure. He boasted, 'Bards train their memories till they can repeat a poem three thousand lines long after only three hearings!'

Instead of labour in the fields and woods, the men made and mended weapons and shields and harness, carved wooden bowls and spoons. Arvenic was building a new chariot, with iron-tyred wheels Cram had brought from Camulodunum. They wrestled, drank, boasted, sang, told stories, invented riddles, stored sleep for the summer. In bad weather, the huts regularly shook with the din of dog- and cock-fighting. They spent good days hunting, and, this year especially, training for war.

Vigorous, hardy girls often learned to fight beside their brothers for a few years – several of the Cheswell women were good fighters. Instead of marrying, a few even took oaths of blood-kin in a war-band of professional women warriors. That became Victoria's ambition. She spent every possible minute wrestling, running, exercising with her Pin, a spear and a small oval shield, presents from Arvenic, till her hands grew hard with calluses and she could hit the target as regularly as the young men who had been practising since they could walk.

The other youngsters of the village still stood off from her, siding with Mac Clanna. He was the favourite of all the tribe, handsome and dashing, loved by all the free women and many of the men; for them, she had done wrong by spoiling his perfect teeth. The slaves loathed and avoided him, but their sympathy did not raise Victoria's spirits, especially as they agreed that the boy she was worried about had run away. Well, maybe he had. She felt like it herself!

Week by week her usual open, if hot-tempered, friendliness withered; she hid her hurt under a sullen face. Aliss and Cram tried to draw her in, but when Cram called, 'Boudicca, can you guess this?' or Aliss beckoned her to join the singing, Victoria would refuse. 'Don't know the songs. I'm no good at riddles.' She would fondle the ears of the nearest hound to hide her awkwardness. They didn't want her, not really . . .

In one way it worked for her. The others tried harder to best her. However, she was tall and strong for her age, and determined never to be beaten. Never. Even nineteen-year-old Mac Clanna, working his tongue in the gap where a tooth had been, urgent for revenge for his humiliation and his damaged looks, found that she faced him valiantly, matched him, and then began to beat him, in their racing or wrestling, or their bouts with wooden spears or swords. It didn't make him like her any better.

Then, in early December, it all changed.

As Arvenic came out of his hut after his morning porridge, stretching and enjoying the crisp freshness of the dawn, some woodcutters bringing in a load spoke to him. He shouted in glee, to wake the village. 'Rouse yourselves, slugabeds! Fat and lazy we are! A sounder of wild pigs down by Three Oaks pool is waiting to greet us. Roast boar tonight!'

As they cheered, he ducked into his hut. Victoria was fidgeting while Aliss rubbed ointment on her latest grazes, while beside her Cram was finishing off his breakfast and joking at her winces. When Arvenic snatched his boar-spear from its peg in the rafters, she demanded, 'Can't I come? I've never been on a boar hunt.'

'You're too young.'

She bristled at once. 'Too young? You made Cram a boar-spear when he was twelve. I'm nearly sixteen. And I'm bigger than him.'

'Wild boar are the bravest and strongest animals in the forest, more dangerous than bears or wolves,' Arvenic warned her.

'You think I'm a baby, or a coward? I'll show you—'

'Don't bully your poor uncle!' Aliss shook her finger, tutting in joking disapproval. 'But she has a point, husband. I know women seldom hunt boar, but it is known – and she is eager to try.'

'It's outnumbered I am! I surrender!' Arvenic raised his hands in mock appeal. 'Don't argue with a woman – and never with two! Aye, aye, you may come, if Cram will lend you his spear.' Lifting down a smaller spear, he glanced at Cram, who shrugged and nodded. 'Very well, girl. Here is your chance.' He tossed the spear to her.

'Oh, thank you!' Victoria's voice was shrill with delight as she clutched the weapon, ready to follow him out, and then paused. 'Thank you, Cram.' It must be hard for him.

'You are the guest,' Cram grunted bitterly. He sighed, gritted his teeth, and made himself smile. 'And a cousin. I wish . . . Good luck. Don't disgrace my spear!'

'I'll do my best!' Victoria headed for the door.

Aliss chuckled. 'Take care, Boudicca! Of your uncle as well as yourself!'

'Of course!' Victoria tossed back over her shoulder. The men boasted about their near escapes, showed off their knotted scars. Last year someone had been killed, his chest slashed open by a boar's tusks. Yes, she'd be careful. As careful as possible, anyway.

She refused a pony. 'I don't ride well enough, if my horse shies I don't want to be thrown right on top of a boar! No, I'll go on foot.'

Considering her riding skill, or lack of it, Arvenic nodded. 'Sensible.'

They trotted down the track, nineteen riders, twelve on foot, with another ten men holding in a score of the biggest, strongest mastiffs, patched and spotted cream, fawn and brindle, black, brown and red. Everyone was talking a bit too fast, too confidently, joking a bit too much. They were nervous too, she realised.

'You people on foot will set yourselves in a line, and wait,' Arvenic instructed her. 'We riders will circle wide round behind them, with the dogs, to spear them if we can, and those that escape us we'll drive towards you. The butt of your spear you'll set solid in a gap between trees, and hold it low and steady. If one charges you, it's the centre of its chest you must aim at, and hold firm. This cross-bar just below your spear-head will stop the beast reaching you. If it backs away – it will not, but if it should – follow it. Only your spear keeps the boar off you; trust it. If you try to dodge, or let go, or let the beast break free of the spear, then even wounded to death it will slash and maybe kill you.'

Exalted with excitement, she grinned. 'What if I miss, or just hit its side, wound it?'

64

He grinned back as he reined away. 'Don't.'

At the edge of a wide clearing they spread out along the front row of trees. Victoria felt annoyed when she was placed far out on the right, the least likely place for a pig to run – but maybe the first time, till she saw how to do it . . . To her irritation, Mac Clanna was next to her. If she made a mistake, he'd be sure to see, and tell everyone!

Silly, if she made a mistake she might be dead, or crippled.

Breath puffed on the frosty air. As they cooled down after the walk, people blew on their fingers, wrapped furred cloaks tighter, wriggled toes inside their sheepskin boots. Grins grew wider, voices and laughs higher.

Mac Clanna pulled the wooden stopper from a ram's horn flask, drank, walked over and held it out. 'A peace-offering?' His smile was wry, but at least he was making the first move, not her. She could accept it, where she could never have asked for some.

She needed both hands to steady the awkward flask. Her spear was in the way; he held it to let her lift the horn. The honeyed burn of the mead warmed her, relaxed her stomach; coughing, she murmured thanks.

He turned away, his head lifted. 'Listen – shouting, and the hounds baying. They're coming. Hush, now, get ready.' He returned her spear and hurried to his place.

Victoria wedged the shaft against a thick root. The hand-long blade was sharp; she had checked a dozen times. Glancing

65

along the line to see what to copy, she knelt and lowered the point to knee height. Yes, better to go in low to catch the belly than glance up off a charging skull.

She strained to breathe against the tension in her chest. Was this really such a great way to spend the morning?

Suddenly, at the far side of the clearing, a dozen animals appeared; black, sturdy, agile, menacing; not as tall as the hounds, not as fat as the swine in the sties, but terrifying. They paused, peering short-sightedly across the open space; then, at fresh din behind, they barrelled forward, small sharp hooves puffing up snow, breath like dragon-smoke, tusks startling yellow.

In a heartbeat they were at spear-point.

The first was struck, and screamed in rage; the others simply raced faster.

One two-year-old boar far out to the side saw Victoria, charged her instantly. No time to think. Hold firm—

The spear actually bent under the first blasting attack. Her arms jolted, her hands slipped, oh gods, the root held, spear-point sunk in the pig's chest, cross-bar flat across the straining muscles, finger-long tusks slashing only an arm's length from her stomach. Its stink, its hot breath, its shrieking gusted into her face. It heaved sideways, backed off, follow it, mustn't let it get free! The spear butt lifted from the root. The beast drove forward again, fast and ferocious, stronger than she was, crazy to kill her as she was frantic to hold it off, spear shaft tucked under her arm now, striving to hold on, keep that blessed shaft of strong ash between her and the flashing tusks—

The crossbar gave way.

The boar thrust forward, driving itself up the shaft, tusks viciously ripping the wood a hand's breadth from her desperate fists – nearer – grazing them – move the hold back – still coming – she'd have to drop the spear and flee—

Suddenly the boar collapsed. She staggered, almost tripped over it. Alive, unhurt.

Gasping, she had time to look round. The whole fight hadn't lasted sixty heartbeats. Men shouting, running, horses galloping into the far side of the clearing, dogs barking and leaping—

Beside her, Mac Clanna slipped and fell, cursing, screaming under the screams of a huge sow, twice the size of her young boar, its long teeth slashing, five dogs attacking it, the side of one ripped wide open but it still held on.

Victoria yanked on her spear till it came free, poised it above the struggling scrum of animals. A handbreadth of the sow's brown bristles showed between the dogs. She jabbed down, and pushed with all her weight . . . At last, the sow's squealing stopped. The howling dogs kept worrying the animal, ignoring the young man beneath – but men were around them. 'Haul the dogs off! Get it off him – heave it this way, roll it! Well done, Boudicca!'

Mac Clanna was unconscious, bleeding. She felt quite sympathetic, since the mead.

'He's not too badly hurt. He is already waking. Gashes on his legs, cracked ribs, some dog bites and a broken arm. He'll live,' his father announced a minute later, with a puff of relief. Formally, he took Victoria's hand. 'Boudicca, you saved my son's life. On your first hunt, too! Quick as a polecat, strong as a bear, smart as a fox, brave as a badger – you deserve your name.'

'The champion of the hunt!' everyone cheered her. 'Cram will make a song about you!'

They had five pigs, one killed by the riders, two by men on foot, and Victoria's two. Grinning, flushed and tipsy with excitement, her heart pounding with the praise, her shoulders sore with approving slaps, her ears ringing with congratulations, she watched Arvenic give the sacrifice of blood and the beasts' hearts to the spirit of the pigs, and to Herne the Hunter, as thanks for success in the chase; and then helped stitch and bandage the hurt dogs, who were given the pig guts as reward for their valour. Two dogs were dead, seven hurt, and a horse lamed; one man would never walk straight again. But it had been a good hunt.

Arvenic was studying her spear. 'Boudicca, has anyone except yourself touched this?'

'No – well, Mac Clanna offered me some mead, and held it while I drank.'

68

'Hmm. The binding looked solid when I checked it last.'
His mouth pursed in speculation, he hunted round to pick
up the crossbar and its leather binding, but shook his head. 'It
must have weakened – or been weakened. But rot, or . . .
I cannot tell.'

Several people had gathered to listen, frowning, exchanging
glances.

Victoria's spine stiffened in fury. What? Maybe Mac Clanna
had cut it? While pretending to be friendly? The treacherous
midden-worm!

But he was hurt, she couldn't kill him right away, and it
could have been accident . . .

No proof. Just like the slave boy. Think.

She shrugged, corking her rage down. 'It could just have
snapped.' She didn't want to spoil their day, or lose the approval
of all the people standing round with their ears flapping.

Arvenic slowly nodded agreement. No-one else mentioned
it. But Victoria noted that many of the friends who helped
Mac Clanna on to the back of a pony to ride home avoided
his eye.

From then on most of the young people of the village went
out of their way to joke with her, include her in their talk and
sport.

Mac Clanna offered flowery gratitude, smiled and smiled
in public; in private, though, as he strutted about, just as
showy and arrogant as before, gathering his friends again, she

could feel ill-will radiating from him like cold off ice.

'What do you expect?' Cram asked when she commented to him about it. 'People hate being in debt, and twice over he owes you – three times, maybe. Once for his life, once because he perhaps tried to kill you by stealth, which is disgusting and shameful, and a third time for not bringing it out into open talk and disgracing him. Of course he loathes you – you remind him of his own lack every time he sees you.'

She hummed thoughtfully. 'Nothing I can do about it, I suppose – except be wary of him.'

A month later, at the winter solstice, Con Veile arrived again for the Yule feast, to offer an elderly mare to the sun god Lugh. While they all feasted on rather tough horse meat till their eyes crossed, the druid praised Victoria's courage and coolness during the boar hunt. She also recommended something Victoria had never dreamed of.

Arvenic insisted Victoria must practise riding, while she protested bitterly, 'I'd rather run all day than ride an hour! No!' All autumn it had been a source of argument, with Aliss and all the slaves laughing at her.

Con Veile was of a different tribe, not mad about horses. She suggested, 'Why not teach her to drive instead? She wants to be a warrior. Teach her, as you would have taught Cram. She could fight from a chariot just as well as on horseback.'

Victoria's jaw nearly bounced off her knees. Chariots were

signs of high rank and wealth. There were only two in the village. But even as she laughed, she saw Arvenic considering it. He felt proud of her, and generous, and suddenly, to everyone's astonishment, he agreed. 'Why not? I'm building a new chariot. She can learn in the old one. And the lads here to train as warriors, too – they can all learn.'

The very next day Arvenic showed off. Before a cheering crowd the kneeling driver took the chariot bouncing round the fields at a full gallop while, light-footed as a squirrel, Arvenic danced forwards and back along the pole between the ponies, swung his long sword round his head, threw spears to hit the target deer-hide seven times out of nine at twenty paces. Victoria was impressed; she could do no better standing still. At last Arvenic jumped down. 'You try, Boudicca!'

Before he could change his mind she was up on the little platform beside his small, skinny driver, Berrin. 'It's like a boat!' she called, clinging to the arched side where the spear-rack was tied, as the chariot rolled slowly forward. 'The leather floor is springy, it smoothes out the jolts, if you keep your knees bent you can stand quite steady.'

Berrin's eyes slid sideways, his wide mouth twitched slyly, the ponies burst into a canter, and the light vehicle bounded high on the ruts. She grabbed wildly, laughing. 'You rotten sausage!'

When it was the next lad's turn, she jumped down happily. 'Thank you, Berrin! That was wonderful!' She hugged Arvenic.

'And you, Uncle – you're wonderful too!' He laughed his high warm laugh, and hugged her back.

The young man beside Berrin fell out within a minute. Everyone jeered. Victoria had done better than that!

As she watched, she frowned. 'I don't want to seem – well, cheeky, I suppose, Uncle. But war chariots seem very – very risky. I don't mean dangerous, but . . . uncertain. In a battle, if one of the horses is killed or hurt, the whole thing—'

'Kill a horse?' Arvenic was quite shocked. 'No civilised person would do that!'

'Father – Rufius – used to describe how Vespasian's men beat off chariots during the invasion, the archers and javelins killing or crippling the horses as your – our – chariots dashed along the Roman line.'

'Oh, Romans!' Arvenic snorted. '*Civilised*, I said!' He beckoned Berric to bring in the chariot to let the next lad have a turn. 'To kill a horse is dishonourable, disgusting, never done! Unless by accident. That is why we have drivers. To fight and control horses in battle at the same time is impossible.'

'No, it can be done, just,' Berrin demurred, overhearing. 'By a skilled man on a broad, level place – a beach, maybe.'

'How often do we fight on beaches? Now that the Romans are here already?' Arvenic demanded. 'No, essential a driver is, to drive you close enough to throw your spears, or carry you past within sword's length in the duel of champions, before the mass of warriors join battle. In that, a chariot is useless. You leap down to fight on foot while he takes the horses back out of the way to be ready for you later. Great honour is due a driver, for he carries no weapons, only a knife to free his horses from tangled harness. It is as shameful to strike him as it is to harm a horse. But, again, accidents can happen. Berrin here is the best and boldest driver in ten villages.' Berrin grinned proudly.

Victoria didn't start driving at once. Berrin heaved a long pine trunk across the top of a wood-pile, like a jolting, unsteady see-saw. 'Jump on. When nine times you can run from one end to the other without falling, Boudicca, and three times of nine spear the target while standing on it, I'll start teaching you to drive.'

For hours every day she and the other learners swayed and tottered, fell off and climbed back up. All her new friends gathered round to cheer and jeer. 'Graceful as a one-legged duck!' 'Steady as a butterfly!' 'What totters and crashes and ends in the ashes? A felled tree? No – Boudicca!' Whenever she let herself be distracted by their laughter and antics Victoria landed among the knobbly wood. Cursing scraped shins and bruises, she learned fast. In only six days she could balance along the pole even when her friends jumped on the other end to try to bounce her off, and throw her spear reasonably accurately.

For weeks then, from dawn till dusk, Berrin taught Victoria and the other young warriors how to start and stop the ponies, get them moving together, and turn them without overturning the chariot or falling out. 'Keep your knees spread – don't pull on the reins for balance! Now, gentle but firm – not so tight . . . Good. Now stand up, I'll drive. Try throwing your spear. You must fight both sides, that's why the driver kneels, so that you don't take his head off when you swing your sword from side to side. No, don't hold on or you'll never learn. Feet further apart – bend forward – lean into the bend—'

Nearby, Mac Clanna and his friends practised throwing spears from horseback, which she could not do. Apparently he ignored her, but she knew he was watching, sneering, envious.

'What happens if the horses go one either side of a tree?' Victoria demanded, wiping mud off her face after one particularly frustrating session.

The spry little man chuckled. 'It's not unknown, lass. But these ones are well trained – by me. It's themselves who know what they're doing, even if you don't. If they don't do what you want, it's because you have not given them the right signals. That is what you must learn. Years it takes to be expert, but they are teaching you how to control them, how to feel what they think—'

'They think?' she sniffed sarcastically.

He tutted at her, hurt. 'Of course they think! Better than some people! They will only work with you, like your hands, if you tell them what to do, with the reins, or a word, or the way your weight moves in the chariot, or even your thoughts. Even though a warrior is driven, he has to be able to drive too, to

74

work as a team with his driver and his horses. Our horses are our friends.'

She sighed. She didn't think horses were friendly, but here, among the horse-mad Iceni, she couldn't say so. At least, though her legs and back ached fiercely, driving was better than riding the beasts.

VI

The year turned faster than Victoria would have believed possible. In no time, it seemed, they celebrated the spring festival Imbole, in February, as the Romans called it, giving a fawn to the young goddess Bridhe in thanks for her white wand which softened the ground frozen all winter by the Cailleach's ice hammer. They were soon in the hungry snap, before any crops were ready to eat, though the stored food was spoiling; they fed the hens on the maggots and weevils they picked out of the porridge oats. However, at last the hens and geese began to lay again, and boys raided duck and swan nests among the marshes. The cows were helped out to eat themselves into skitters on the new green shoots of grass in sheltered corners. The first lambs and kids were born, and several babies, nine months after the Beltane feast last May.

Twenty days of downpours in March flooded the fields, stopping the spring ploughing and the chariot-driving, keeping everyone cooped up like broody hens. When at last the rain stopped, every soul in the village exploded out of doors into a bright, frosty dawn. Victoria decided, as usual, not to ride out hunting, and cheerfully wished her friends good luck as the cavalcade charged whooping among the trees in a flood of excited dogs. She slipped on her new boar-hide jerkin and boots, the only things she had ever managed to stitch neatly, and called Cram. 'Berrin's busy with a foaling mare, he says the horses need exercise and I can take the chariot out along the track if I'm careful. Put that harp down, forget your plinky-plonky for once and come along!'

'Plinky-plonky? Who started the dogs howling with her caterwauling last night?' Cram demanded in exaggerated offence. As she threatened him, laughing, he fenced with her for a moment with his crutch, and then pretended to flee, squealing in mock terror.

The ponies were eager to run. 'We'll take the south track. How fast can we go? Get along, there! Stop dodging the puddles! Leap the trees!' She cracked the reins, urging the ponies faster than she ever had before, and farther.

'Careful, Berrin said!' Cram yelled, clinging breathlessly to both sides as the little chariot bounced along the overgrown path, crunched through the puddles, tossed up showers of icy spray and frost-rimmed leaves. 'Is it Camulodunum you're heading for? Or the moon?'

'The moon!' Victoria howled.

'We're certainly in the air as much as on the ground!'

They shrieked in delight at the rush of speed, the freedom – till suddenly she hauled on the reins, staring forward. 'Whoa, there! Whoa back! Cram, look – a stranger! Outlaws?'

'I don't see anyone else, or hear, do you?' Cram peered all round. 'A single man's no threat. Gods, he's filthy! And limping, in trouble.'

'Here, hold the reins.' Victoria drew up beside the man and jumped down. 'Greetings!'

He leaned wearily on the side of the chariot. 'Greetings to you. Morian I am, son of Fornor, headman of Dun Fonith. I bear a word for the thane of Cheswell.'

'My father,' Cram told him. 'Climb in, we'll give you a lift.' They helped the young man up to sit in the back of the chariot, sighing in relief, nursing one arm. 'What happened to you?'

'My horse fell and broke a leg. I was a little damaged, and also with running.'

As Victoria climbed back in, she puffed in respect. 'Your feet are all bruised and bloody. Your message must be important!'

It was.

That noon, to all the village crowded into Arvenic's hut, Morian told an appalling story.

'A man came to Dun Fonith yesterday, one of the king's friends. He had lived at the palace in Venta – the great hall, with nine rooms, each fuller of treasures than the one before. He was wounded, near dead. He carries a message from Queen Boudicca to all the Iceni. You know King Prasutaeg died last summer.'

'It's no trouble at all that will cause. His chief wife, Boudicca,

78

will rule until their girls marry. Four or five years, probably,' Arvenic explained to Victoria. 'One of their husbands the thanes will choose as king. For now, no-one dares argue with Boudicca!'

Wearily, Morian shook his head. 'The Romans . . .'

'What about the Romans?' Cram demanded as Morian hesitated.

'Hush, boy, don't interrupt a queen's messenger. We know Prasutaeg left half his lands to the Emperor Nero in Rome,' Arvenic declared. 'Nearly everyone does it, it stops the Romans claiming it all.'

'They are claiming it anyway.'

Everyone hissed dismay except Cram. Not abashed by his father's disapproval, he lurked in his corner, grinning in dark glee, muttering, 'War! War at last!'

'Boudicca would never allow that!' Arvenic protested.

'That is the worst. The Procurator – er—'

'Catus Decianus,' Victoria prompted him. Everyone glanced at her. Well, of course she knew who he was, did they expect her to be ignorant, or hide it?

'Yes. That son of a diseased stoat. The Queen returned from honouring her husband's head in the sacred grove, and found Decianus arrived in Venta, with five hundred soldiers – looting the palace. Slaves were already emptying the treasure chests. A woman cannot rule, in Roman law, the Procurator said – though Queen Cartimandua has ruled the Brigantes to the north for twenty years, with Roman help! But Decianus says that since the king died, the Iceni land all belongs to Rome. All. Not just half the king's own farmlands, not even all of them, but every thane's land, every farmer's, every hand's breadth, every horse, every ox and goat, every grain of barley, every river pearl, every man, woman and child, free, serf or slave, like a conquered nation.'

'Conquered? Roman law? What have we to do with——?'

'No. No, be silent, let the man finish!' Arvenic's bellow hushed Cram's vivid cursing, the clamour of disbelief and anger.

'Boudicca cursed him, "The Morrigan strike you down, you and your men, and leave your heads for the maggots! Your mean little souls will be foot-scrapers and arse-wipers for the souls of the heroes!" '

They roared approval. Morian lifted a hand. 'Decianus had her flogged.'

He closed his eyes against their appalled faces. 'Her men could do nothing, not with Roman swords at their throats. After fifty lashes still she stood defiant. She told the Procurator that every man of the tribe would seek vengeance. She would reward the man who slew most Romans, even a slave, with her daughters as wives, and he would be the next king. So –' in the shocked silence, his breath rasped '– Decianus told his slaves to rape the girls. There, in front of their mother and everyone. "Who will marry them now? Let all the people know that

Rome is Master!" the Procurator announced. And the Romans laughed. The queen and her children, and her friends and servants, they thrust into a horse-pen to sell as slaves, but some broke out. Boudicca and her daughters are free. The messenger had a sword-stab in his ribs.'

Arvenic was chewing his moustache in fury. 'The Roman Governor ordered this?'

'No, he is west, in Deva. One of the officers protested that General Suetonius would be angry at this stirring up trouble, especially now. While the legions were needed to attack Mona, he meant. But Decianus sneered, told him if he was afraid to become rich, to go back to Rome.'

'Rich! That's all they care about! The Morrigan curse them all!' Cram was spitting in fervent fury.

His father hushed him again. 'The druids? What did they do?'

Morian shrugged. 'Hid. You know the Romans hunt and kill them. But the Queen Boudicca sends out word. She calls a meeting at Thetford, at the new moon.'

'Two days. To Thetford?' Arvenic mused. 'Far – but we can make it in the time.'

Aliss nodded. 'In an hour we can leave.'

'No. Only the thane. In secret, in case spies tell the Romans.' Morian half smiled. 'There would be much to tell them. Messages have gone out to the other tribes in the north, also. To call them to war.'

Like his son, Arvenic was passionate with rage. 'This will start the revolt the druid spoke of. Thane or farmer, free or slave, warrior or pig-herd, we are ready! We will destroy the Romans, give their heads to the gods, or drive them back to their stinking city, out of our land!'

Cram led the cheering.

Victoria joined in, for a minute. Then she stopped, and thought; and slipped outside.

Someone touched her shoulder. She jumped, her hand on her sword, but it was Cram. He jerked his head to draw her over to the horse pen, where they sat on the poles of the fence.

He was briskly intense. 'We've been itching for years to blood the spears and become warriors again. This insult to the queen, and the threat to all of us – well. Would you hold back, if your mother had been treated so, Boudicca? And yourself?'

'No!' Victoria protested. 'I know you have to fight – we. *We* have to fight. It's just . . .'

'You have friends in Londinium.'

Victoria snorted bitterly. 'Some of them I'd slaughter myself, like the bullies who attacked you. But the good, kindly people, like Dio, and Bron – and what about Mother, married to a Roman? And my sisters, and Rufinus, they're half Roman. What about them?'

Cram grimaced. 'You are going to have to decide, cousin. To stay torn like this will rip you to tatters. One side or the other!

But for your mother and sisters – they are our own people.' He set a comforting arm round her shoulders. 'Father will rescue them. Don't fret.'

To please him, Victoria nodded. 'I'm with you!' But she didn't think it would be as simple as that.

Arvenic returned five days later, with a tale that Cram set to music.

'Great was the meeting, glorious the gathering, shining the silver, glittering the gold,

Bright the banners, standards of fame, horse of Iceni, wolf's head and crane,

Helmets and horses once proudly vaunted, bronze of shield-bosses, swords iron cold,

Weapons once hidden now flashing and flaunted, bright in the light to bite once again.

Lugh our sole witness in the arena, spying eyes only the ravens he sends.

Prayed the High Druid, the great Olc Custeddin, prayed for the gods to turn us their ear,

Prayed for their favour, prayed for their fortune, force to destroy Roman rule in the end.

'Tall in her chariot, vital and splendid, red-haired and tempered, Boudicca, queen,

Gold at her throat from her royal forefathers, gold at her hair her helmet's gleam.

Knelt at her knee white fawns of the red deer, desolate daughters, dark-eyed with tears.

Turned she away from us, slipped off her gown, showed us her skin from the neck to the hip,

Dark as the night with bruises of beating, netted and scarred with the slash of the whip.

Wept we in sorrow and anger and fury. Boudicca wept not, storming in rage.

'Will we bow down to the conqueror's legions? Soft pay their taxes and kneel as their slave?

Mothers and daughters, our wives and our children, will we watch helpless, wringing our hands,

While they are starving or beaten or ravished, stolen by Rome who conquers our lands?

Will we all labour to build up their temple to Claudius, Emperor, never a god!

Will we die trembling, toothless and old, leaving unhonoured our head-bones to rot?

Weep weak as water while druids are dying? Sell our young men to their legions for fee?

Creep in the shadows that once were our homeland, serve in our own lands – or will we be free?

Cowards or dotards, once-great Trinovantes? Careless of shame and their women's reproach?

Will the Iceni cower to Romans? Will you surrender, or fight for your right?

Follow your queen to the glory of battle, leap out from shadow into the light?

Are you as fierce as your valiant fathers, welcoming joyful a foeman's approach?

Not as a queen do I speak, but a woman. Net, god of battle, answer my call!

Hear me, Andrasta, goddess of triumph! Strike down our enemies, force them to fall!

Glory and honour, rewards for a hero. Mine either freedom or sleep in my grave.

Freemen, fight with me, feel with me, follow! Rather I'll die than live as a slave!'

Fiery and fierce with the flame of her fury, lifted on loyal love, hearts soaring high,

Weeping the warriors swore to avenge her, drive out the Romans or die.'

The singing harp strings stilled to silence.

Exalted by the swelling surge of excitement, inspired by the song, by pity and ardour for the wronged queen, by hatred for tyrants, Victoria joined Aliss and all the people of the tribe, and cheered till her throat was hoarse; while Arvenic tugged the ties off his peace braids, and tossed his head till the long fair locks flew free for any enemy to seize to take his head, if he dared!

VII

A month later, on the planned day, the day of the summer Beltane festival, Victoria fidgeted nervously among the foot-soldiers of the village, a tiny handful of the horde that surrounded Camulodunum. Beside her Cram leaned on a spear for a crutch, and behind them hovered Aliss and half the women and older children, ready to finish off the wounded – and loot the city. The chariots were out in front, just hidden from the city by the outer edge of the forest. Victoria wasn't yet good enough to drive or fight in one, or even ride a horse in the brilliant ring of warriors.

Chariot fighters, riders, foot warriors proudly wore their finest clothes, their richest jewellery, offered as a splendid trophy that challenged their enemies to come and take it. They bristled with spears and swords; most had iron-banded helmets, many with bird wings or horse-hair plumes like the Romans. Their oval shields were painted in swirling patterns and fierce beasts, studded with metal bosses to strengthen the wood. Some had chain-mail armour, which Cram disgustedly condemned as new-fangled and cowardly.

No-one had escaped to warn the town as the army gathered round it. Victoria had not been in any of the swift, merciless raids on the scattered farmhouses, but by now she was used to the sight of bodies, and of trophy heads dangling round the ox-carts.

She glanced at Cram, and found him glancing at her. Her stomach was turning somersaults in her belly. 'Scared?' she asked.

He bridled. 'Of course not! A warrior fears nothing!' His voice was high with nerves.

She grinned wryly. 'Yes, so am I.'

He had to chuckle. 'Father says if you're not afraid, you can't be brave. It seems twisted, but I suppose he's right. It just feels so – so weak, to admit it.'

'If there's nothing to fear, there's nothing to be brave about. Or if you're not, then maybe you're just too stupid to realise what's happening.' She rubbed her belly to ease it, and heaved a deep breath. 'Never mind, it'll start soon, and we'll both win our heads. Look, there's the queen!'

In the distance, just visible, a red-painted chariot moved forward from the trees. In it, wearing a gilded helmet and a blood-red and green checked cloak, Queen Boudicca gestured – releasing a hare, Victoria knew. If it ran towards the city, it was an omen of victory . . .

A glinting arc; the queen had raised a spear, and swept it forward. Cheering, howling war cries, the gaudy tidal wave of the tribes raced across the fields towards the first houses.

Cram limped along as fast as he could, but was soon left behind by the Cheswell fighters. Victoria stayed with him; somebody had to guard his back.

The outlying farmers were slaughtered unawares, often by their own Trinovant slaves, but when those nearer town realised what was happening, the retired soldiers and their families fought back fiercely. Three times Victoria came on a skirmish, but to her frustration her comrades' long, swinging swords were unhandy in the narrow streets, liable to stick in plastered walls or bounce off stone ones, and dangerous to try to pass; she could never get close enough to exchange actual blows with an enemy. She lost her spear early; the man she aimed at grabbed it and carried it off. 'Oh, Morrigan curse him! Cram, stop laughing!'

Victoria and Cram paused in a small open square for a drink. A ring of children's heads had been perched like spectators on the wall round the well-head. She suddenly threw up.

'That shocks you?' Cram asked curiously. 'We must kill baby rats as well as grown ones.' He hauled up a bucket of water, casually knocking the heads aside.

'No, it's just the smoke,' she protested. The attackers, or perhaps the Romans themselves, had set many houses alight. She mustn't let him think she was soft! 'But children aren't rats, not even Roman ones.'

'They grow up,' he shrugged. 'It's not a boar hunt, it's war.

We let piglets go, so that we can eat them later, but not foes. A warrior should be kind to comrades, but not enemies.'

'I suppose so.' She drank gratefully, forcing her stomach to settle.

'Whoo, I'm sweating like a pig just with running after Romans!' Cram rubbed his bad leg, emptied the bucket over his head, and grinned through the waterfall at Victoria leaping forward–

Three men with axes!

He grabbed his spear, thrust half-blinded – his short leg unbalanced him – he stabbed up from the ground, felt his spear go home, yelled in glee – a blow on his left hand knocked away the spear – ach, curse all Romans . . .

As he scrabbled for it, Victoria straddled him, slashing Pin desperately about her, screaming in battle fury, stabbed again and again, curved back from an axe swinging at waist height, it slammed into her belly, only her heavy jerkin and belt buckle saved her from being gutted – thank you, boar! – don't waste time thinking about that now! Pin's too light against axes, can't keep them all off! An axe crashed into her shield, she stabbed wildly at the axe-man while his weapon was stuck, he fell back dragging the shield from her hand – Morrigan help me! – but he backed off . . .

The surviving Romans turned and fled.

'I got one!' Puffing, Cram sat up. 'I've killed my first man!' He beamed at her in triumph, stood up to free his spear, twisted the axe out of her shield and chopped at the dead man's neck – but suddenly his face fell comically as he stared at his left hand. 'I've lost two fingers!'

'Careless!' Victoria joked, and then realised what he was saying. 'Truly? Oh, no, Cram! Will it cripple you?' His eyebrow twitched ruefully. 'For playing, I meant, stupid; I'm so used to your limp, and you manage so well, I just never think of it.'

'Thank you.' Staring at the blood, Cram shrugged. 'Ach, well. Just the outside half of my hand, and not my playing one either, thank Ceridwen.'

'Here, I'll bandage it for you.' She bent painfully to cut strips off a dead woman's gown, and rubbed her stomach. 'Oowah! No, it's just a bruise. It'll be spectacular tomorrow, though.'

'Winning my head is worth a couple of fingers!' Even in his pride and joy, he thought of Victoria, and looked up at her sympathetically. 'Yours got away – but you'll get one soon! Whoo, that was sudden, eh? Thank you again, cousin. If you'd not been there . . .'

She chuckled as she wrapped his hand. 'Saving you is getting to be a habit.'

He grinned back. 'Well, not a bad one, don't stop! It's a debt I'd rather have than not.'

'Your face must annoy Romans,' she suggested. 'Like it does everybody else.' He stuck his tongue out at her.

'Well fought, both!' Arvenic's voice made them jump. He was leaning against the well, applauding them, his sword arm dripping blood. 'Aye, as well I wasn't more Romans, eh? Pay attention all the time! Cram, your hand does not hurt now, you're too excited to feel it, but it soon will, and nothing hurts more than a wound to the hand. Go back to the camp. No, don't argue. Three things a warrior needs: his hand, his heart, his head. Short of half a hand, as well as limping, you cannot defend yourself. Your share is done; leave some for the rest of us! You can start making your song about your first trophy.' He cocked his head. 'How many have you killed?'

'A dozen, at least!' Cram boasted proudly – exaggerating was expected.

Victoria wouldn't spoil his triumph. 'About six.'

Arvenic eyed her quizzically. 'Indeed?'

'Well – no. Only a couple wounded, so far. Ach, one! But I'll win my head yet!'

'Of course!' he assured her. 'Bring some of that cloth to bind up this gash for me before it makes my hand slippery. Lernis is dead, and old Con Druor. The Romans are fighting well, but we're driving them back to their temple. We'll set it ablaze for our Beltane sacrifice, and see can their God-Emperor save them then!'

Victoria nodded to a bundle by Arvenic's feet. 'What's that?

'An officer's helmet.' He kicked the bundle, which clinked. 'Very fancy. He did not want to lose it, but I won the argument. And his head, too!' They laughed together.

91

'I saw Mother a while ago, with a full sack,' Cram said, wincing at last as he moved his hand. 'She looked happy.'

'So she should, the plunder here is enormous.' Arvenic looked round swiftly at a clatter of hooves, but relaxed. 'Our own lads.' He waved and whistled, frowning. 'A prisoner? The queen said to take no prisoners.'

Mac Clanna and three friends cantered up, screaming and hooting in triumph, their ponies' manes hung with heads tied on by their hair or strings through their ears. The man hauled behind them by his tied hands wore a tribesman's tunic and trousers, but his hair was cropped short in the Roman style, and tears in his blood-stained clothes showed armour beneath.

Mac Clanna reared his pony right in front of Victoria, to make her flinch. She didn't. 'See the mighty Roman!' he exulted, waving a long wig on his spear like a banner. 'Sneaking off in disguise, the coward!' Gloating, he poked the Roman with the spear. 'We'll see how loud you can scream tonight! Tell him what I say! I will flog him, as our queen was flogged, and burn out his eyes, and slice his skin from him for the druids to make magic! Tell him!' Their friends cheered and made suggestions.

Suddenly, under the blood, dirt and bruises, Victoria recognised . . . 'Certinus? Is that you?' Her heart shrivelled. She knew the tribes often tortured enemies, and she had been rather dreading it, even after what had been done to the queen and her children, and her own parents, and hundreds of others over many years, she knew. But a friend – this was appalling.

He peered at her from eyes swollen to slits, head reared defiantly, wiping blood from his mouth with his tied hands. 'What stinking savage knows me?'

'What does he say?' Mac Clanna demanded.

'He is an optio – no, a centurion, of the Second Augusta Legion. His name is Certinus.'

Mac Clanna's eyes lit up. 'You know him? You know him! I knew you were a spy!'

'That's foolish, if I was a spy would I admit to knowing him? He's a friend of my father! I've known him for years! And he's not a coward!'

'Then why was he fleeing from the battle? Ask him!'

'I was ordered to go, bitch, to carry news to Londinium, to the Procurator, to send up the Second and drive you savages back into your swamps!' Certinus snarled. Bleakly, Victoria translated for him. 'There are only five hundred soldiers here, you're fighting civilians and women and old men, but we'll hold you till the legions come! I've killed over twenty of you! Any Roman soldier can do the same!'

Jeering, they beat him till he fell to his knees, grunting at the blows and kicks. He spat blood at them – and his bruised eyes suddenly sharpened. 'Victoria? Vicky?'

Her insides seemed to tear apart. What should she do? Whose side was she on, really?

93

Certinus seemed to read her thoughts. 'They're planning to torture me, aren't they? Victoria, I'll not beg. But I found Dio for you, when you wanted to learn to fight. So, who will you fight for? Will you help them hurt me? Or help me?'

Mac Clanna said the same. 'What is he saying? Begging for his life? Well, Boudicca – prove now whose side you are on! Is your heart truly Iceni?'

One side or the other. Arvenic, who had saved her at risk of his family; Cram, her cousin, ruthlessly determined to drive out the Romans; gloating Mac Clanna; her new friends, screaming hate for all Roman tyrants – like Certinus, her friend for ten years, kneeling defiant in the dust, his eyes on hers . . . What to do? She couldn't help him! She couldn't do anything!

She couldn't do nothing!

She could not save his life. But . . .

Certinus closed his eyes. He knew, he was making it easier for her . . .

A sudden fast sweep of her arm, with all her strength, before any of them could move, slashed Pin through his neck. As the blade swished, she was sure he smiled. Then his head toppled and thudded to the ground, his body crumpled in an astonishing torrent of blood.

Oh, gods, what had she done?

Mac Clanna's screech of disappointment – and triumph – jerked her mind from the blood, the remorse. 'I knew it!

Roman at heart! She saved him!' He slid to the ground. 'Boudicca, I challenge you, you traitor, I'll slay you, you renegade—'

Victoria gulped. She had saved Certinus from torture. Now she must save herself.

Spurring her ready temper, she stuck her face right into Mac Clanna's, till his tattoos and war-paint danced before her eyes. 'Saved him? I killed him! But no, I'd not let you torture him! He deserved better! He helped save Cram in Londinium!'

'You mean he saved the Roman boys!' Cram protested angrily.

Arvenic spat. 'You prefer a Roman to your tribe. You disappoint me, cousin's daughter.'

The rest raged at her. 'Raised by Romans – spy – can't trust her – traitor!'

In a tide of angry guilt, she raised Pin. 'Come on, then, all of you!'

They brandished spears and swords, shouting – and suddenly fell silent.

A red chariot with black ponies drew up behind her, bearing a tall, impressive woman, her red cloak bright in the breeze, her red hair wild under a gilded helmet. Queen Boudicca.

'You fight each other instead of the enemy?'

Arvenic stepped forward to explain. Boudicca listened in silence, but her grey eyes drifted away, stared over their heads. When Mac Clanna started to shriek accusations, she lifted a hand. 'This is nothing. Nothing!' Her voice, rich and commanding, was harsh with anguish. 'Word has just come from Mona.' She paused, her mouth tight. Poised to cheer, they stopped, in sudden dread of her news. 'Mona is destroyed. In vain, all in vain, the druids' strongest spells, fiercest fighting. The heart nemets are cut down and burning. Dead, slaughtered they are, all, all, and all the wives and husbands, the children, the babies, all slaughtered, save a few who fled to bring us word.'

'But – how?' Arvenic was aghast. 'How could the Romans succeed? Our gods—'

'Maybe their gods are stronger.' She shrugged. 'Maybe we should surrender, submit.'

'No! No!' The young men howled with him. 'Never! Death to the Romans!'

'What about her? What about Boudicca?' Mac Clanna yelled through the din.

'If we cannot trust her –' The queen paused, her bitterly implacable expression changing. '– Your name is Boudicca also? I will not create an evil omen, by killing another Boudicca now. Especially when it means "victory". Arvenic, I will see her later.'

Grimly, she nudged her driver to move on.

'Back to the wagons, niece. Cram, see she gets there.' Arvenic raised his long sword, his mind already re-focused on the battle. 'Death to the Romans!' They all raced off towards

96

the main fighting round the towering temple in the town centre, only Mac Clanna turning to yell back a threat and a curse.

Dully, Victoria pulled a handful of weeds to wipe Pin. She had been so eager to fight, had dreamed of taking her first head, of proving herself as a warrior; but this was her friend Certinus's blood . . . And nearly the blood of her Iceni friends.

Were they still friends? No, not now.

What a mess she had made of her life. If she had obeyed her father like a docile, obedient Roman girl, she'd be married, safe in her own house.

Or beaten to death already, maybe. You never knew the future, till you looked back on it.

Well. She had done it. Now she had to deal with it.

'His head is yours,' Cram said, nodding at Certinus's body. 'If you think he's worth it.'

'No-one gets my friend's head!' she snarled. Her shoulders slumped. 'That's not – not the Roman way.'

He shrugged, and watched, silently disapproving, wrapping his own trophy in cloth from the woman's dress and tying it to his belt while Victoria dragged Certinus's body inside the nearest house and then reverently carried in the head. She lit a broken stool at the charcoal stove, and carried it out to the street to toss on to the roof. 'Mars Ultor, here is a brave, honourable soldier. Receive his shade kindly.' The flames caught readily in the thatch, as a funeral pyre.

Her hands were shaking so much she had trouble picking up her shield.

His mouth wry, Cram held out his own hand. 'Mine too. Remember?'

He lifted Arvenic's sack with the helmet, and jerked his head. 'Come on.'

They walked for a while in silence. At length, Cram sighed. 'An act of mercy. I know, Boudicca. But a mistake it was. Not only disloyal to us, friendly to a Roman enemy, but soft-hearted. Not our way. You didn't think. Again. A warrior must be ruthless. Mac Clanna will fight you tonight, or tomorrow.'

'No, he won't.' Victoria was confident about that, at least. 'He knows I'd beat him. He can only win one out of four fights with me at practice. And for real, I'd fight harder. I don't need to worry about that.'

'Worry?' Again, Cram sighed. 'A true warrior would look forward eagerly to the duel. And Mac Clanna has challenged you. He must fight, or be called a coward.'

'So?' Victoria's chin rose. 'I'll still win! What I did was right! Would you have tortured the man who saved you?'

'Of course. He was a Roman.'

His ruthlessness took the heart from her. She should have known, though.

Cram was scowling. 'It's spoiled this day is for me. Not just my fingers, that's nothing. You. How you have betrayed us – betrayed me. I'll make no song about my first head. Not now.'

They had fought round to the south of the town, and had a fair way to go back north to their wagons, past groups of chariots waiting for their warriors to return, and wounded men being carried from the battle. Eventually they came across the Cheswell chariots, with an unconscious man lying in the oldest one, the one Victoria had learned to drive. Berrin greeted them with relief. 'Boudicca, will you drive Terrec here out to the camp, and then bring the chariot back? The other drivers have gone off to join the fighting, and somebody must stay with the horses.'

Cram nodded. 'We'll see to it, Berrin.'

Victoria needed to break the awkward silence as she drove back the couple of miles to the farm-house they had captured. 'You can get someone to lead the horses back, I suppose.' Cram didn't reply. 'They're eager to run. They've been resting all day, of course.'

'I wish I had been.' He sounded really despondent.

At the camp, Victoria was going to jump down when Cram laid a hand on her arm. 'Stand still.' The slaves and wives left in the camp cheered at the news of victory and the head Cram displayed, sympathised with the lost fingers, carefully lifted the wounded man out to his bed under one of the ox carts. Then he climbed down, finally hissing at the pain in his hand, and stood looking up. 'Boudicca, I must tell the camp all about the fight. You take the chariot.' As she opened her mouth to argue, he snarled quietly, 'Think, for once in your life! Will the tribe ever trust you again? Will you ever be happy or at ease here? What should you do?' His voice held a note of more significance than his words.

She gaped. 'Are you saying—'

'I am saying you should consider your future actions very carefully. Think! May the Three Mothers guide you to the right decision.' His mouth was pinched with exasperation, at himself as well as at her. 'You are my cousin. I brought you here. You helped me. So. I pay my debts.' He hesitated. 'I cannot lay a geas on you, that is the gods' work, speaking through druids, or through a king. But as a future bard I set this obligation on you; you will not do anything to harm your family. Good luck.' He turned away.

Shocked, Victoria shut her mouth again, and turned the ponies to drive back to Berrin.

He couldn't mean what it sounded like? That she should run away? Again?

He paid his debts? She had saved him. Was he trying, without actually saying it, to save her? Giving her the chance to save herself, to escape, even though it was dishonourable – for both of them . . .

Think, he had said. She tried to.

Even if she beat Mac Clanna, would the tribe ever truly accept her now? Arvenic – Aliss – Boudicca? No, never.

Who would warn Londinium, now Certinus had been caught? Who would save her family? She had seen a battle, now; Arvenic might try to find his way to their house among the thousands of attackers, but could never do it, not for certain.

Father might kill her . . . No. Her jaw jutted; she fingered Pin's hilt. No. But she'd not let her family be killed if she could help it, either. Cram had solemnly ordered her not to allow harm to come to her family — and yes, that meant those in Londinium as well as Arvenic and Aliss and him. She would go and warn Londinium herself.

Travel at night, again? Alone? Wolves and bears, spirits and gods and ghosts?

Certinus's ghost?

Ach, the Morrigan take all wolves and bears, and robbers! She still had mother's amulet to protect her from spirits, and Certinus's ghost, if it could see her, would be grateful and help her. This was the right thing to do. In her Iceni clothes she'd pass freely through the army of Iceni and the other tribes. A new, smooth army road ran straight all the way from Camulodunum to Londinium. She'd be there tomorrow.

She turned the ponies to head south, her belly aching, her head throbbing, her tears almost blinding her.

VIII

Victoria's amulet protected her from ghosts, but not from grief for Certinus. Nor from fear. Even when she had to stop to rest the ponies, she could not relax, Mac Clanna might be galloping after her with all her friends . . . His friends.

When she finally arrived in Londinium, after a day's fighting and fasting and a night driving, she was exhausted and aching.

That didn't matter. She had to warn everybody!

But wherever she went, the response was the same.

The sentries at the fort gate; the centurion in the guard-hut; the senior centurion, thirty-one years in the army, the most experienced soldier in the camp; the traders in town; they all scoffed at her. The commander of the cohort – a plump, spotty young tribune, not much older than Victoria, just out from Rome – was typical, when she argued her way in to see him: 'Three thousand Roman veterans beaten by a gang of hairy-faced barbarians? Rubbish. Camulodunum burned? Folly. See the Procurator? Don't be silly. You're insolent – clear out! Quiet, you! Soldier, give this bitch a good thrashing! The guard's there to keep lunatics out, not send them in!'

She was lucky; the soldiers didn't flog her with the crippling lead-spiked whip used on criminals, they just walloped her with their spear-butts.

A small crowd of merchants in the marketplace, including her old sword-fighting teacher Dio, all jeered at her news. Finally she screamed at them, 'All right, don't believe me! But I swear to you before all the gods that the next people coming down the road from Camulodunum will be Boudicca's army!' They scowled and snarled, and turned away in contemptuous dismissal.

Her anger died. Her shoulders slumped, and she rubbed her suddenly painful bruises. 'Oh, Three Mothers, I tried.'

The only man left, Dio, looked disgusted. 'You an' your imagination! We all thought you was dead – I sacrificed a dove for your spirit. Never thought about how we'd feel about you drownin', did you?'

'How would you have felt if I'd stayed and married Drogo, as Father said, and he'd killed me? Would you have felt happy then?' she demanded.

'Who's to say he'd've killed you, eh? Just your pig-headed, big-headed fancy. If girls could choose their husbands they'd only pick the pretty boys. Would that be better? O'course their dads know what's best for 'em! Women obey their husbands, daughters obey their dads, it's the way things are! Girls marry men they don't know all the time!'

'Just because it's traditional doesn't make it right!'

'Ach, there never was any arguin' wi' you! Get off home!' He spat and stamped off.

It was the only place left to go. The place she most wanted to go – and most feared.

Warriors wear a brave face, even if their guts are curling. Especially then.

Bron was in the shop, more like an ancient bloodhound than ever. She hugged him, while a heavy-built young man, a new assistant, blinked sullenly. She had had hours to think this out. 'Yes, it's really me, Bron, I just pretended I'd drowned. I knew you were watching me. I'm sorry for upsetting you, but I had to get away without anybody following me.' She spoke clearly enough to be heard through in the living-room.

The old man's face broke into watery smiles. He actually started to sniffle. 'Miss Vicky – young mistress – you're really here – oh, thank the gods – somebody ran in and said – so they know – but I didn't – oh, go on through, miss! Oh, thank the gods, thank the gods!'

Her mother came hurrying into the store-room, to exclaim in astonishment – with a hidden wink – hug and kiss her. 'You're well! You're hurt!'

'Just bruises.' Warriors never moaned.

'Come through, let me look at you . . .' Weeping with joy, Mara drew her into the kitchen.

A plump, sly-looking girl was kneeling at the grindstone, staring open-mouthed. From his hanging cradle in a corner, little Rufinus regarded her with a worried frown, rattling and chumbling the bones of a lamb's tail. 'Hello, Rufi! Oh, mother, how he's grown! And you, girls – I'd scarcely know you, you're so tall!' Rufinia and Aegyptilla, after a moment's staring, recognised her with delight and swarmed all over her.

Rufius Aegyptus, in his high-backed chair, welcomed her with a glare, his mouth twisted. 'Victoria. You disobedient, unwomanly, impious monster!' He did not rise; she was taller than he was, so he sat enthroned to overawe her. 'The gods will punish you. You cared nothing for your mother's grief. You ignored the gratitude you owed me for rearing you as my own. You let us think you dead, callously left us to grieve for you while you wandered off with your barbaric kinsfolk. And now they've thrown you out you return, begging to be taken in again.'

She glared right back at him over her sisters' heads, grimly holding back her anger. 'I left because you were going to force me to marry a man who would kill me – how much did you care for *my* feelings? Or *my* life? I'm not begging, and nobody threw me out. I've come back of my own free will, to warn the town. All the Iceni and Trinovantes and half a dozen smaller tribes are risen against the Romans. Camulodunum is destroyed—'

'Folly!' he interrupted her, and scowled at the slave girl who had started to whimper. 'Stop that noise! And you two!' At the harsh tone, the little girls dropped away and backed off to their mother. 'Yes, Victoria, we've heard of your tale. A silly girl's stupid, wild, unjustified, hysterical exaggeration. I'll hear no more of it! No, not a word!' Mara was patting the slave girl's shoulder in a comforting way. Rufius huffed scornfully.

'Father —' it was habit, and she'd use anything to help convince her step-father '— listen to me. Just listen. Let me tell you exactly what happened, and then you can judge!'

Mother nodded approval. 'That's sensible, dear. No drama, now!'

Grudgingly, Rufius nodded. However, he dismissed her story. 'Some houses are burned in a riot, and in the smoke you see the same men several times and imagine crowds. And you admit you left in the middle of the fight. No, I don't believe in this full-scale rebellion. A village or two, maybe, some hot-heads, yes, but whole tribes — no. I'm sorry Certinus was killed, but that's fate. He went up to Camulodunum to guard a load of wine I sold to the Governor's office. Fate. The veterans will hold off the rioters till Cerialis brings the Ninth Gemina south. One good legion can thrash any number of bawling barbarians. In any case, Suetonius will soon bring his two legions back from Mona — you heard about that? The druids were screaming and dancing on the shore, sacrificing babies to cast their black spells, we heard. It shocked the soldiers, but they recovered, and either sailed across the narrows or the cavalry swam beside their horses, fought their way to take and hold a landing, and wiped them out. Good riddance!'

'Even their children?'

Her father said exactly what Cram had. 'You have to kill young rats as well as old ones.' Victoria felt sick all over again. Rufius glanced at Mara, who was biting her lip. 'Your young cousin, what's his name, Con? Was he there?'

'Cram. No. The druids told him to stay away till it was over.'

He sniffed at Mara. 'There you are, then, you can stop fretting, he's safe.'

'No, he's not. He's with his father, attacking Camulodunum.'

Mara sighed. 'And Aliss, and half the other women, too? Husband, this is serious—'

'Don't you start! No! The girl is no blood of mine, she's a savage, unruly and hysterical. I should whip her for scare-mongering! She'd never have done for Drogo anyway. Her sister was a much better choice.'

'What?' Victoria's jaw dropped. 'You married Aegypta to Drogo instead of me?'

'At least she considers what is good for the family!'

'And you called *me* callous! She's only thirteen, you—'

'No, no, Vicky, stop! You have it all wrong!' Mara's smile was wry. 'She suggested it herself. She said Drogo was a fine rich man, it would be a pity to lose the partnership, she could handle him, and – most important to her, I think – she'd be the first of her friends to marry. I was doubtful, but she was determined, and it seems she was right. Drogo visited us on his last trip, just a few days ago. She's thoroughly enjoying her new

107

life, ordering her own household, three slaves, a big house and garden, seeing to all his affairs while he's away. She's well and happy. We can believe it; Drogo was better dressed and neater and politer than I've ever seen him.'

'Three Mothers! Well done, Aegypta!' Her fury melting, Victoria couldn't help laughing.

Rufius sniffed. 'Well indeed.' He huffed a deep breath. 'To please you, Mara, and for no other reason, your daughter may stay here. She can sleep beside Prestia in the kitchen. For one month, no more, unless she can convince me that she will either obey me like a daughter, like a decent woman, and wed the man I choose for her – if I can find one, now – or earn her own living. Though I can't think how!'

'I'll not impose on you, Rufius Aegyptus.' Stiffly, from reviving anger as well as pain, Victoria stood up. 'I'll sleep by my horses.' She bowed slightly to Rufius's glare, kissed Mara and her sisters, and walked out, listening to the row starting in the room behind her.

Bron was helping the assistant put up the shutters. 'This is Servic, he's new.' The young man bowed, his smile broad but, she felt, insincere. 'Master'll be out all day tomorrow,' Bron whispered. 'Your belly hurts? Here.' He slipped her a bottle of liniment from the shelves.

Next morning, after her step-father left, Victoria went home. She had to describe all her adventures in Chcswell, especially the boar hunt, to general wonder and applause, before Mara sent the girls out with the slave girl Prestia, and settled to discuss the war. 'I believe you, my dear, every word. I've been expecting trouble, ever since that Seneca man – he's the senator who lent the nobles all that silver – started demanding it back. I couldn't think why he should do that, so unexpectedly, if the Romans were not going to start some new assault on the tribes, but I couldn't convince your father. They say the Roman officers here owed him money, too, so they were looking for loot to pay him off – there's no proof, but that could be why Decianus was so greedy, so suddenly. We can go to Aegypta in Burdigala. I'm planning my packing already. But I can't do much without Rufius knowing, or I'd hire a boat now and – what's that noise in the street?'

They stiffened at the tramp of heavy boots outside, and an exclamation of dismay from Servic in the shop. Two legionaries stamped in. 'You're that girl brought news o' Camulodunum? Right. Come on – you're wanted.'

'Who by? What for?' Victoria fought to stop her voice squeaking. 'Is there more news?'

'Move!' Without answering her, they shoved her out and marched her off up the road past staring, worried, muttering groups. In one doorway a woman was screaming, sobbing.

Yes, she thought. Her news had been confirmed.

This morning, instead of being lackadaisical, the sentries were alert and edgy. The senior centurion was awaiting her in the guard room. 'The Procurator wants to speak to you. Mind your manners!' No word of apology for the beating. Well, he was Roman.

Catus Decianus was a plump, soft man of about thirty, with plump, soft lips, now twitching in nervous irritation, and the baggiest eyes Victoria had ever seen. The young tribune, looking resentful, stood behind him at his desk in his big offices, while an older man, obviously an ex-soldier, slumped exhausted and bloodstained on a stool before them.

The Procurator waved a hand at the man. 'Publius Narvensis says Camulodunum is destroyed. When he left the temple was burning and he thinks no-one else escaped, or was even taken prisoner. I believe you brought word of the tribal rebellion yesterday. I was not informed.' He glared at the tribune, who stared accusingly at Victoria as if it was her fault. 'So. What can you tell me now?'

Victoria licked her dry lips and told her story again, while the Procurator's plump, soft fingers pleated the edge of his purple-bordered toga. He seemed more baffled than afraid or guilty. 'But why? They were settled – at peace! Why ruin it to avenge a hulking virago?'

'Queen Boudicca was – is – a sacred person, Catus Decianus, the tribe's link with the gods, the heart-stone of the whole Iceni people, even more than the king,' Victoria tried to explain. That was exactly why he had mistreated her, of course, to break the Iceni spirit. 'Besides, they enjoy fighting, they don't want peace. And you – we –' curse it, there it was again! '– we

110

have taxed everybody to build the great temple to Claudius the god, that the tribes all see as an abomination. We've driven the Trinovantes off their land to give it to the veterans, enslaved them – the Iceni don't want that to happen to them, too.'

Decianus shrugged. 'They're not Roman citizens. They're barbarians!' he expostulated. As if that meant they were worthless, beneath consideration. For him, of course, it did. He huffed angrily and rubbed his plump, soft face. 'How dare they? Who'd have expected . . . They must realise . . . How they think they can succeed . . . Oh, Jupiter! What will they do now?'

Victoria shrugged. 'I don't know, sir. My father says the Ninth Gemina will destroy them. But they are so many, and they've re-armed recently, in secret, they'll be confident, and more tribes joining them now – and Legate Petillius Cerialis – well—'

'Exceedingly brave officer, sir,' the senior centurion put in, as she hesitated. 'Impetuous, even.' His face and voice were properly impassive, but his contempt glinted through. The green young tribune frowned, not quite sure enough of himself to check the vastly more experienced man.

'Foolhardy, you mean!' The retired veteran from Camulodunum didn't need to watch his words or his expression. 'Mars Ultor, the man's an idiot!'

The Procurator jerked a hand up to stop him, smoothed his toga and waved Victoria away. 'Wait outside, girl. Saevio will want information about the tribes and their leaders later.' The tribune nodded uncertainly.

She stopped to retie her boot strap just outside the door, beside the clerk at his desk there. Elaborately ignoring each other, they strained to hear the talk inside the office.

The Procurator's voice was high with stress. 'You think the tribes could – er – delay Cerialis?'

'He'll underestimate them,' Publius Narvensis snorted. 'He wasn't here during the invasion. Vespasian's the man we need now – he may be Vespasian's son-in-law, but as a soldier, Cerialis isn't fit to tie his bootlaces! He'll come racing south from Lindum, no scouts, all strung out – I've served under him, sir, I know. Look, Decianus, I've seen the tribes fighting. Delay Cerialis? They'll wipe him out. As they wiped out my family, and Camulodunum.' His voice was harsh with exhaustion, pain and scorn.

'Um. Saevio?'

'Sir?'

'What's your plan?'

'Me? Er—' The young tribune was taken aback by the question. 'Er – can we – er – defend Londinium? All my men will fight to the death—'

'Naturally, sir. But no walls, sir. Only six hundred men,' the centurion broke in firmly. 'Not against fifty thousand. Message to the legion commander, sir? And the Governor?'

'Er – yes. Yes? Er . . .'

The Procurator lost patience. 'Of course! Send riders at once. Tell egate Poenius Postumus to force-march the Second here, immediately.' He cleared his throat. 'Governor Suetonius will return with his legions from Mona shortly, and in the meantime I have, of course, every confidence that the Ninth will wipe out the tribesmen, but we must – er – ' He paused to select the right word. 'We must reassure the locals. And organise a fast ship to be ready to leave in a hurry. A galley, not one that can be held in harbour by a contrary wind. It is time for the collected taxes and debt money to be sent to Rome in any case, and I must report this trouble to the Emperor.'

Victoria just had time to dodge aside as the centurion, disgusted by his superiors' uselessness and desertion, scarcely waited for the young tribune's nod before snapping a salute and marching out. 'Clerk! Get your notebook in there. Urgent messages!'

Victoria tried again to persuade her friends among the merchants to believe her, but came home disheartened and frustrated. 'It's no good. They'd not listen, just drove me out. Some even cursed me.'

'They don't want to believe you. They're afraid,' Mara said. 'They'd have to accept that great Rome can be beaten. So they won't listen, not in public. But some are already leaving, quietly.'

'Remember Varus's four legions in Germany, that Father talks about? They were wiped out, every man. And it's going to happen here!'

Mara hugged her. 'Let's hope not. Or maybe – if the Romans win – oh, I don't know! I'm like you, I don't know which team to cheer!' She sighed. 'We'll go and pray for peace. Though whether the gods will listen . . . Rufinia, get our shawls. Take Tilla's hand, please, Vicky. Prestia, stop snivelling and bring the baby. We'll buy some doves and go out round the temples.'

They were not the only ones. The temples to the eastern Mother Goddess Isis, to Jupiter and Mars, Neptune and Vesta, were all crowded, their carved roofs and pillars sweet with incense, noisy with prayers. The priests were busy, sacrificing steadily, birds, lambs and goats, and a pure white ox from the town council as a whole to the gilded statue of the God-Emperor Claudius. Doves had doubled in price. Nobody would meet Victoria's eye.

Next day Victoria and Mara crossed the ferry and walked three miles south to the nearest nemet to pray to the British gods too. Local gods were generally ignored unless they were considered a source of opposition to the Romans, who often simply accepted them as a version of Roman ones; they saw Lugh as another name for Apollo, god of the sun. The Tamesis valley tribes had been peaceful, and so far this grove was untouched. Victoria had been there once before, when Mara went to pray for a son. Now, they found that it too had been busy with sacrifice. The trees were draped with bright cloths. Heads – nine animal, two human, but old, taken long before – were hung or spiked on the branches, and coins and little figurines, and scraps of lead or tile with prayers and curses scratched on them, were thrust into cracks in the bark or thrown into the sacred pool.

Below the ancient face roughly carved on the hugest oak tree, a baby's body lay on a mossy root red with its blood.

Mara swallowed. 'For peace, or for victory?' she whispered.

They poured their offering of wine and perfume, made their prayer, and hurried home.

IX

Bron warned Victoria, 'Be careful, young mistress, or they'll arrest you!' She had fought with the Iceni, after all; how far could they trust her? She was as popular as a leper. Twice she even had stones thrown at her, though – perhaps fortunately for her as well as the throwers – she didn't see who did it.

Her mother just shrugged. 'Nobody loves a bearer of bad news.'

At least she could get to know the family again, while Rufius was out during the day. Frail little Aegyptilla was a nervous, shy child, whose squint was disconcerting. Though small, Rufinia was noisy, boisterous; 'Just like you were, dear,' Mara sighed.

'And look how well I've turned out!' They laughed together.

The maid, Prestia, was good with the toddler, Rufi, but Victoria disliked her. 'A bad bargain, and a bad influence on the girls,' Mara agreed. 'Rufius accepted her and Servic in payment for a debt, to help with the work when you and Aegypta left. He's from Gaul, across the Narrow Sea, and her father was a merchant from Hispania who went bankrupt. This is the third time she's been sold, and I'm not surprised. She whines constantly and acts stupid, she's slipshod and sly, and terrified of spiders, though everyone knows they're messengers of the gods. Servic's lazy, and insolent when Rufius is out, and Bron says he gambles. I'm sure they both steal, even more than most slaves. She says things are lost, and the takings are down in the shop. I'd sell them, but Rufius likes Servic, he's all smiles and helpfulness when the master's about, and he's strong when you can get him to work. Ach, well. We'll catch them yet.'

Victoria had paid a silver ring to stable her ponies with a carter's oxen and mules in a barn on the edge of town, and chain her chariot among the carts in the yard. She slept in the loft above them, to guard them as well as to keep out of Rufius's way. Pin, handled casually but firmly, convinced the stableman that she wished to sleep alone.

However, every night she tossed restlessly. Not from the scratchy straw; from her scratchy conscience. Whenever she fell into a doze, she dreamed of Arvenic, saying, 'You disappoint me!' Or of Certinus's face, smiling and closing his eyes to let her strike him more easily. She shuddered awake, over and over. She sacrificed to Certinus's spirit, and was certain that he forgave her. But still . . .

One night she started awake as usual – but *not* as usual. Certinus had not been smiling, but shouting. Warning her? Why? The animals below her were stamping as rats rustled through the hay – her horses were still uneasy indoors–

A faint chingle of harness being lifted, and a whisper . . .

Not rats.

Gently, rolling over and muttering as if in her sleep, she drew Pin. Then, howling the Iceni war-cry, she rolled to the edge of the upper floor, leapt down into the stable below all ready for battle, twisted her ankle and crashed down, cursing. A heavy shadow tripped over her. Something hit her head, half dazzling her with a flash of stars. In the flickering glow of a little oil lamp she made out two forms, slashed at one, heard a frightened yelp . . .

Nobody was hitting her. The lamp had fallen. Victoria stopped yelling and shoved herself to her feet to snatch up the lamp and stamp the flame out fast, before it spread through the straw.

A man fled, limping. A woman crouched sobbing in a corner. The animals' kicking, neighing and braying created such a din that she thought the whole town must waken, but as they calmed, nobody came in. Where was the stableman?

Victoria held the light high to see the woman's face – and almost squeaked in astonishment. 'Prestia?' Whimpering, the slave girl stared at her hopelessly. 'That man – that was Servic? The rat, to leave you here! Oh, stop wailing!' She huffed in exasperation. 'You wanted to run away, I don't blame you – but why not just run? Why try to steal a horse? You could be crucified for that, didn't you know?'

Prestia wailed helplessly. 'Oh, please, miss, don't tell! Please, please! I got two silver sesterces, you can have them! I never done nothing wrong before, never! We never have no luck,

118

thought you'd not come after us, not with the tribes coming, an' the stable door was open, see, we never thought until we saw that, we could get further away, see, Servic's idea it was, but you hurt him, see, an', an' your little sisters, who'll look after them, oh don't get me crucified, beg you, lady, I love them like me own—'

'So much that you were running off to leave them in danger!' But she was so miserably mean and wretched, holding out her pitiful little coins . . . 'Oh, put your money away, and wipe your nose before you drown us all in snot!' Frankly, Victoria didn't want anything to do with the wretched girl and her weasel lover. She sighed. 'Go home, Prestia. Straight home, and stay there! And stay clear of Servic. You can do better than that cowardly thief.'

'Juno bless you for your mercy, lady! I'll never do nothing like this again, swear by all the gods!'

As the girl bent to pick up her bundle of clothes, she also lifted a cudgel her lad had dropped.

That was what she had twisted her ankle on, Victoria thought – and then realised the girl was edging towards her . . . Deceitful, lying, treacherous bitch! Victoria hefted Pin. 'Drop that!'

'What, this? Oh, miss, you don't think – I'd never – oh, miss! Never, not when you been so good!' Prestia looked shocked and offended, as if an attack while Victoria was off-guard was the last thing that would enter her mind. She glanced sideways through lank hair, her voice suddenly ingratiating. 'I don't suppose – in kindness, noble lady – to save our lives, just – you're not Roman yourself – you could let us take a mule? Not one of your ponies, of course, but—'

'Jupiter, you have a nerve! Get out, and think yourself lucky!'

The girl scurried out without a word of thanks, as the stableman lurched in, carrying a strong smell of ale. He swayed gently, peering round at her. 'Frien's, Vicky? Tha's nice. All be frien's. Frien'ly cuddle, eh?' He lurched towards her. She firmly fended him off. 'Not frien'ly. Li'l Vicky, not frien'ly at all.' Heaving a reproachful sigh, he reeled off to drop, snoring already, in his bed in the corner behind the door. Victoria had to laugh, while she dropped the bar across the big doors. The next thieves might not be so easily driven off.

Next day, Prestia was in the kitchen as usual, head down, flinching from everyone, never raising her red-rimmed eyes, apparently thoroughly cowed and obedient; but somehow Victoria felt her spine shiver whenever she turned her back on the girl. Servic limped round the shop, whistling over-innocently; and winking insolently at her as if she was an accomplice in his attempted theft.

She had been, she realised. And having kept quiet so far, she could say nothing about it now, so he had a kind of hold on her. The Morrigan – no, Mars! – take the pair of them!

About noon a couple of cavalrymen raced in from the north, down Ermine Street. Maybe the Ninth had already wiped out the rebellious tribes? But they didn't shout news of a victory, and one had a bandage on his thigh.

A slave cleaner carried out the appalling news; the Ninth had been ambushed. Cerialis had escaped with some of his cavalry, but all the foot soldiers had been killed. Three thousand of them.

Victoria borrowed a length of chain from the shop, to tie up her chariot more securely.

An hour later, the worried people spilling out over the roads, ignoring business, arguing, panicking, weeping, were shocked again. Four army carts left the camp gates under heavy escort. They drove down to the river bank, where the largest ship in the river was under armed guard. To boos and jeers, dozens of chests of silver were loaded aboard. The taxes of the entire province were being carried off to Rome, as usual – but by the Procurator in person.

All the merchants and bankers, tradesmen and their families, all the people who had come from all over the Empire to find fortune in this new town beyond the edge of the world, twenty different shades of skin, watched, cursing and pleading in twenty languages, as Decianus and his clerks embarked for safety, away from the war their greed had started. 'Seti curse you for a cowardly thief!' 'I'll pay a thousand sesterces for passage to Gaul!' 'Please, please, take my little boy with you!' The soldiers had to draw their swords to keep back the crowd.

121

Mara did what she could to prepare for flight with Rufinus and the little girls, but her husband snarled at any talk of escape; 'I trust the legions!' He refused to allow Mara and Bron to pack any of his stock, or hide the household silver, but stubbornly went on with his business, snapping up bargains. 'I've bought Ferox's warehouse and shipyard at a quarter their worth last week!' he boasted. 'They're all cowards, like Decianus! I'll own half Londinium before I'm done!'

Next morning, not long after dawn, fifty weary horses clattered down the road from Verulamium, the bigger city north-west of Londinium. A cheer rose from the citizens as they recognised the leader, the Roman Governor himself; 'Suetonius! Suetonius Paulinus! You'll save us!'

At noon, though, soldiers marched through the streets sounding trumpets, calling everyone to assemble on the open ground before the camp gate for a speech from the Governor. He had ridden out round the town once, with the young tribune and the senior centurion, ignoring shouted questions; apart from that, the camp had been shut tight since he arrived, not even a slave coming out to whisper news. Rufius came back in to collect Mara, and, since she was there, Victoria. He was full of satisfaction. 'We'll see some action now! Suetonius is a soldier's soldier! His legions will finish that rabid she-wolf up north, double-quick!'

They had expected to wait for quite a time, knowing the usual delay of the Procurator's arrangements, but they had scarcely arrived at the back of the crowd when the Governor appeared. The camp gate stayed shut. He stood on the walkway above, from which spears or arrows could be showered on attackers, and looked down on the townsfolk as if they were indeed an enemy.

Suetonius's voice was harsh. 'Citizens of Londinium! You have heard of the burning of Camulodunum, and the loss of the Ninth Gemina, apart from Petillius Cerialis himself, and some of his cavalry.' The crowd moaned at the confirmation of the dreadful news. 'The tribes are moving south. Our scouts say they will be here tomorrow.' Someone shrieked, but was hushed. 'I have ordered the legions under my command, the Fourteenth Gemina and the Twentieth Valeria, to come south as fast as they can. However, they are weary after the hard fighting on Mona, and are far away. Even my cavalry could not reach here before the tribes. I came ahead, on our best horses, to see what could be done for you.' He drew a deep breath, his face grim. 'I have consulted my officers, and inspected the area. I have no good news for you. Londinium has no walls, no defences apart from this one small wooden fort. The single cohort here cannot hold thousands of barbarians. There is nothing I can do.'

'What about the Second Augusta?' Rufius yelled from the crowd.

If possible, the general's face grew even sterner. 'Their commanding officer Poenius Postumus has sent no reply to the order from the Procurator to come at once. I must assume he is not coming – at least not in time to help.'

'What, then? What can we do?' yelled an appalled voice.

'Flee.' In the dead silence, his voice carried to the farthest slaves at the back. 'The cohort here is leaving shortly, to march north-west to Verulamium, to join the legions coming south, to make a sufficient force to meet and, gods willing, defeat the rebels. Those of you who can, may come with us, under our protection from scattered raiders and robbers using the rebellion as excuse to attack Romans. You may prefer to go elsewhere, to Gaul, or to the loyal tribes south or west – you might head for Isca Dumnoniorum, where the Second Augusta are stationed. You may stay and fight to defend your homes, or hope the rebels will pass by. Though they were heading south yesterday, they may not be coming here. They might scatter home with their loot from Camulodunum, as undisciplined savages do, or turn west direct for Verulamium. You might be safest to stay here. With us, you may be heading into danger, not escaping it. The decision is yours. But we, the soldiers, are leaving. Those who will follow us must come now, or travel alone and unguarded.' He stared out over their heads and gave the formal salute. 'Long live the Emperor, and the Senate and People of Rome!'

The crowd exploded into a frenzy of tears and lamentations, begging him in the names of fifty gods to stay, to take them all, to wait at least for an hour, to save them! But he had already turned away and disappeared down the steps inside the little fortress.

Victoria and Mara exchanged one glance. 'Get your chariot. Run!' Mara hissed.

Luckily, they had been near the rear of the crowd, and could get away before the full flood of people overwhelmed the streets, seeking mules, carts, boats, any means of transport. Rufius and Mara ran home, to – finally – pack; Victoria raced as fast as her bad ankle would carry her for the stable and her precious horses.

The carter was already selling a mule for twenty times its normal price, and people were pouring up the lane after her. She slipped in past the carter, dragged her ponies from their stalls and out to the rapidly filling yard.

'Five hundred silver sesterces for them! For one!' a man yelled in her ear. 'A thousand!' yelled another. When she still shook her head, tying the last knots of the harness, they shoved her aside so hard that she fell, and actually began to fight each other for possession.

Picking herself up from under the blind tramping feet, she drew Pin, while her ponies started rearing, alarmed by the din and the grabbing hands at their bridles. One man fell back, his jaw broken by a flying fore-hoof. The other backed off from Victoria's sword and the frenzied ponies.

'The Morrigan take you all!' Panting angrily, cursing her sprained ankle, she gathered up the reins, leapt into the chariot, raised her sword to drive back a frantic woman with a child in her arms, slashed the hand of a man who tried to drag her out, stabbed another, and lashed the ponies. They objected violently. Their plunging forced the panicking mob back and let her steer towards the street. Wildly rearing and biting, they broke a way through the bedlam of curses and screams. Sweeping Pin about to keep off people trying to leap aboard, Victoria somehow managed to haul the ponies aside into the narrow lane behind Rufius's yard. Fortunately no one followed her.

'I'm here!' she yelled over the wall. 'Mother, bring the children out!' The ponies were still plunging; she jumped down, yelped at the stab of pain in her ankle, and hurried to their heads to hold them steady. 'Hurry!' They heaved her up and down, on the edge of flight. 'Hurry!'

Rufius led the family out of the doorway, carrying little Rufi tied in his wicker chair. Behind him, Prestia held a grizzling Tilla in her best shawl, Rufinia was jumping around screaming in wild excitement, Servic held a large bundle of clothes and blankets, and Mara was stuffing a silver bowl into a clinking sack. 'I can't take everybody, not all at once,' Victoria called, struggling to hold the ponies still. 'Father, if you bury the silver, I'll take Mother and the children out a few miles towards Verulamium, where the army's going, and leave them somewhere safe. Then I'll come back for you.'

Her stepfather tied the baby's chair to the side spars, inside the chariot. He snorted in disbelief breathing hard but grimly controlled. 'Hah, you'd just – oh.' He stopped and bit his lip. 'Yes, yes, very good. There's a farm about six miles out where I buy pigs, Mara knows it, you can drop them there.'

'Stop wailing, Prestia!' Mara snapped. 'You and Servic, and Bron of course, will come away with your master, we won't desert you!' She handed Servic the bag and climbed into the chariot. 'Listen, there are the trumpets, the soldiers are leaving. Hand me up Rufinia and Tilla.'

While the slave-girl turned, snivelling, to call Rufinia, Rufius slung the draw-string of the silver bag over his head and shoulder and took the reins from Servic. 'Go to their heads, Servic. I'll hold the reins while you get in, Victoria.'

Rather gingerly, Servic walked forward and took hold of the ponies' bridles. Victoria started round towards the rear of the chariot. Instantly Rufius jumped into the chariot and whipped the free end of the reins across the ponies' rumps, yelling, 'Go! Out of the way! Go, go!' Servic flinched aside as they leapt forward.

Staggering, clutching the side of the chariot, Mara screamed, 'Stop! Stop! The girls!' She grabbed for the reins.

Victoria started to hobble and hop after the chariot. Hopeless, but she had to try. 'Stop! Stop, you cowardly bastard!'

'Let go, stupid!' Rufius back-handed Mara across the face. For a moment they struggled in the rocking, bouncing little shell as it careered along the narrow lane; then he elbowed her

127

just as a wheel jolted across a stone. She toppled backwards. 'Mara!' He reached for her, but the ponies were bolting. A wheel ran over her leg. As the chariot whirled round the bend, his knee was holding steady the little chair with his precious son, the bag with their valuables was swinging on his shoulder, and he was not looking back.

X

An hour later the hysterics were over, and the cursing. If Rufius lived more than an hour, seventeen gods were deaf. They had calmed the children, more or less; pulled Mara's broken shin straight and splinted it as best they could, and bandaged her cuts.

Victoria had limped out to try to fetch the army doctor, but was too late. She watched the representatives of Roman power march out through the resentful crowd. Women and old men desperately begged the six hundred men of the cohort to stay and protect them. Paulinus and his small band of cavalry, leading the retreat, had to force a way through a hail of pleas, curses and not a few stones. The cohort's trumpeters and drummers, once the Procurator's pride, marched silent today.

Another crowd followed them: half the population, all those who had horses or mules, donkeys or ox-carts, or could hire or beg a place on one, or were strong enough to walk thirty miles a day. Rufius was in there somewhere. As they trickled away north, Victoria felt sick. What would happen to those who were left, too weak or sick or old or scared to move?

They would die. Soon, within a day or two, the tribes would arrive, and take no prisoners. Their gods would be glutted with the heads of those who stayed. Many people were fleeing to hide in the countryside, trailing wailing children or pathetic bundles, hoping to be overlooked; most would be caught, or die of starvation or exposure, or be robbed and killed by the local tribesfolk, other refugees or runaway slaves. Few would find friendly natives willing to risk sheltering them.

She returned home depressed, near despair. But she mustn't show it . . .

'Let's have some wine, mother! The best stuff, that Rufius keeps – kept – for the officers. No sense in wasting it. No, the good cups, Prestia – for all of us, you and Bron and Servic too.'

Mara gulped her wine gratefully. 'There's a honey cake in the larder. Give the girls a slice each. Why leave it for the Iceni? Take it outside, girls, play with your dolls. On you go, Finia, I'm fine now.' The little girls trotted out, consoled by the treat. White and shaky with shock and pain, their mother was still determined, 'Now. This is my home. I'll stay here. I'll dress in Iceni clothes, and pretend I'm one of the wives, out for loot, and I've had an accident. If they think I'm with their army, they'll not harm me.'

'There are other tribes,' Victoria protested. 'They'll not know your tattoos. Maybe they won't even speak Iceni. And they'll not stop to think, not in battle frenzy.'

'Well, *you* suggest something. That's the best I can think of.' In irritation, Mara moved carelessly, winced and cursed.

'You can't stay!' Victoria rubbed her face. 'But – but we can't leave, either. Not with your broken leg and my twisted ankle. That rotten—'

Her mother sighed. 'I suppose he feared you'd not come back for him.'

'Huh! He'll be reborn as a worm in the belly of a toad!'

Servic, sullen and unsmiling since Rufius deserted them, gulped his wine. Without waiting for permission, he poured himself more. Bron glanced at Victoria. She was already alert. Although Servic was a coward, he was big and strong; if drink made him rebellious . . .

'Bron, you and Servic and Prestia could take the girls after the soldiers,' Victoria suggested.

Servic and Prestia cheered up instantly, but Bron looked doubtful. 'Unless the tribes do head for Verulamium first.'

Frustrated, Mara beat her fists on her knees – and yelped in pain. 'They might not come here at all.'

'This is – was – the Procurator's headquarters. They'll come. How Rufius could . . .' Victoria shuddered in fury, but corked it down. 'No, no time for that now.' Think . . .

'Ach, what's best? Vicky, couldn't you go with them, love? If we made you a crutch?'

'I'm not leaving you alone, mother.'

'But you're the same as me – they may not stop to listen to

you. And what if Mac Clanna, or any of the other people from Cheswell recognise you? Arvenic will keep me safe.'

'If he gets here first. If he's still alive. If he hasn't gone home like the Governor said, with his loot.' Victoria was gloomy.

'Oh, he'd never do that!' Mara coughed as the wine caught her throat.

'Prestia, get Mother some water, please,' Victoria said. Sulkily, Prestia lifted the lid of the well in the corner. As the leather bucket splashed down, Victoria and her mother suddenly gazed at each other in simultaneous inspiration.

'We'll hide in the well!' Victoria's face was alight.

'Nobody will notice it in the corner! Bron, you can cover it with a mat.'

'It's just wide enough to take us both, and the girls!'

'Bron, and you two, you'll have to go and hide away from the town – I'm sorry, but there's just no room for you in here too. They'll not stay long. They don't like towns.'

'Right, Mother! When they've looted the place, they'll leave. Even if they burn the house, we'll be safe down there. And then you come back, and we'll think again.'

All afternoon the barred doors and shutters rattled repeatedly as old folk or slaves, abandoned by their families, drunken with ale from the deserted taverns, tried their luck for loot or food. Bron guarded the front door, Victoria the yard. Luckily, when they shouted, the would-be raiders left.

Whining constantly, Prestia baked a lot of bread and roasted three geese. 'I'd rather eat them than leave them. If the Iceni eat them, they'll be feeding the family in a way, but I'd still grudge them!' Mara joked.

The long wine barrel that lined the well, holding the river gravel from falling in at the sides, was just wide enough in the middle for them all to squash in, and Mara and Victoria to take turns to squat with a child sitting on their knees. Servic dropped crates of pottery into it to build a rickety platform just above the water level.

'That's good, Servic.' Mara nodded. 'Now, it's still too deep for me to haul myself out. Run down to the wood yard and find us a ladder.' He glowered; he might just run off and leave them all. She smiled up at him. 'And when you get back, I'll give you and Prestia letters of manumission, and some silver to keep you when you leave. Rufius didn't take it all!'

Legal freedom? His scowl disappeared. Almost eagerly he slouched off, and after enough time to make them worry lugged back a slim tree-trunk and a sharp axe. 'Dio has gone with the army, mistress. His ladders are all too big, anyway, but I'll chop notches in the sides of this to make steps, and that'll fit in the well.'

'That was good thinking!' Mara praised him. Victoria and Bron watched him even more carefully, as he cracked open another amphora of wine. With that axe . . .

However, Mara carefully jollied the two slaves along, with jokes and and occasional firmness – 'No, we'll need the axe, but you can take two kitchen knives, and a whole roast goose.'

Laden with food and blankets, with five silver coins and their precious certificates of freedom, they were ready to leave just before sunset. Victoria opened the yard door and checked for them. 'The lane's clear, all quiet, just drunks singing in the tavern next door and some noise down towards the river, fighting over a boat, probably. Good luck!' They staggered away without a word of thanks or farewell. 'Good riddance!' she murmured after them.

She settled the heavy bar in its sockets and limped into the house. 'I wonder what he stole while he was out, and stashed ready to lift? Ach, the Three Mothers guard them, I suppose, Prestia's harmless, at least. When will you leave, Bron?'

'At dawn,' the old man said. 'I've filled a bag with food. The tribes don't like moving at night for fear of spirits, so if they're coming tomorrow they'll probably arrive just before noon.'

Mara agreed. 'Bron, you've been a treasure, worth your weight in gold!'

'No, no, mistress, only my duty!' He blushed, while Victoria hugged him.

'Far more than that, Bron. I sometimes think you love me!' Mara joked.

Bron blushed even deeper. 'Oh, no, mistress,' he mumbled bashfully, turned away and busied himself with his packing.

Mara half-smiled, and frowned to stop Victoria making a joking comment as she realised it was true . . .

After a sleepless night, Bron was ready to leave at the first shade of light in the east. As Victoria helped Bron hoist his bundle to his shoulder, Mara called the little girls. 'Stop jumping about! Come and wave goodbye to Bron, he's going away for a while. Yes, he'll be back soon, like your father.'

Victoria hoped so, for all their sakes; she would have to provide for them if Father didn't return.

'Good luck, Bron. The Three Mothers watch over you,' Mara said.

He kissed her hand. 'Thank you, mistress—'

There was a crash in the street, a clatter of hooves and wheels, a shrieking war-cry, voices screaming. Victoria gasped. 'Oh, gods, it's them! Already! Come on, Mother, into the well! Tilla, Rufinia, come here, fast!'

Tilla grabbed Victoria's legs. 'Vicky, won't the fishes eat us?'

'No, no, there's no fishes in a well! But you have to be very quiet, or the water goddess will suck you down! Not if you're good!' she stressed as Tilla's face crumpled, ready to howl. 'You do as you're told, play hide-and-seek quietly, and we'll all be safe. All squeezed up and a bit cold, but safe. Yes, you can take your doll!'

Mara, gasping with pain and surprise, sat down on the edge of the well. Bron and Victoria knelt down, each took a wrist and lowered her to stand on the crates, her head an arm's length below the rim. The girls were lowered into her arms. 'Hush, now!' Victoria hissed to them. 'Bron – maybe you could slip out the back?'

The old man smiled at her and handed her his bag of food and blanket. 'Someone is chopping at the gate. Go down now, my dear, and the gods bless you and keep you safe.' She kissed his cheek and slithered on her stomach over the edge, to catch her good foot on a notch of the ladder and reach for the lid. 'I'll do that,' he told her. 'Now, not a sound, whatever happens.'

His smiling face was the last thing they saw as the lid was lowered over them. Tilla whimpered. 'Quiet!' Mara whispered sternly. When the little girl couldn't stop, she held her tight and clasped a hand over her mouth. 'Sh!' Rufinia looked up at Victoria and shook her head hard, lips tight shut to show she'd not make a noise. Victoria lifted her and cuddled her. Their thundering heartbeats must be making the whole house tremble – the whole town . . .

Above, shouting. Bron yelling, 'No – no!' The thud of a fall shaking the lid above them. Footsteps, a laugh, someone cursing. Crashing of pottery and glass from the shop. Victoria shuddered, seething in frustrated fury. But she must control herself . . .

After a while, silence in the house; in the distance, shouts and screaming.

Slowly, they all relaxed. A faint haze of light filtered down through cracks between the boards of the well's lid, just enough for them to see each other's eyes gleam wide, to ease into a crouch, to slide Mara's leg – with silent wincing – down the side of the crates to let her sit, cuddle the children more gently, and shiver.

'Bron?' Victoria whispered. 'Bron!' No answer. The light from above came from the sides of the lid; something dark lay across the centre. Bron's body. Something she was glad she couldn't see dripped slowly on to her shoulder.

The light grew, to noon and after. There was no noise, no movement above them, apart from an occasional patter of footsteps as a looter checked the house. But they were not found; Bron was protecting them in death as he had in life. She prayed for his spirit's safe journey to the Land of Youth.

They opened the old man's food bag. 'Mother, this goose is tough!' Victoria complained.

'Sorry, dear, I'll do better next time.' Rufinia actually giggled. 'That's my brave lass!'

They played in whispers with Tilla's doll, and told stories and riddles; anything to keep the children quiet. Rufinia dozed, and Tilla. Victoria wished she could; she was cramped, cold and miserable. But a warrior didn't complain.

Then a sound . . . Victoria remembered it, from Camulodunum. She nudged her mother. 'What's that roaring? I'm afraid . . .'

'Sh.' Mara eased Tilla on her lap. 'Nothing we can do. We're safe here.'

'Of course!' Victoria smiled confidently, but her heart ached more than her arms, holding Rufinia close to shelter and warm her. Yes; the rebels had fired the town.

Everything was wooden. The walls were wattle and daub, inter-woven staves of chestnut or ash between heavier timbers that supported the upper storeys and the roof, all plastered thick with clay. But when it grew too hot the clay would crack and fall off, and the wood would burn as fiercely as the thatch above. Then it would all crash down on top of them.

Bron's body would help keep some of the heat off – gods bless the man! But enough? And the smoke? They should be all right, but if the gods decided otherwise . . . They might be better off trying to run – but they couldn't, not with mother's broken leg. Oh, curse Father – no, Rufius!

Mara's eyes were wide and anxious. Though she tried to keep still, not to alarm the children, they woke, catching the fear, smelling the smoke, starting to whimper.

Victoria smiled down at the little frightened faces. 'If we keep the lid above us wet, and ourselves, we're safe. Hot, but safe.' Cold, but safe, she had said, only this morning . . . She scrabbled with a foot for the leather bucket and tossed water up on to the wood above them.

'Oh, horrid cold!' Rufinia complained as it fell back on her head.

'Well, work with me, pass me up the bucket – we're so tight I can't bend down – sh!'

Footsteps thudded in the room above. They froze.

A woman yelled something; Victoria knew the voice. Bron's body was hauled aside, and the lid crashed back.

The four crushed together in the well peered up, blinking in the light.

Let it not be Mac Clanna . . . No. Victoria only knew one of the four faces that grinned down at them; Prestia, pointing at them, betraying them, terrified but triumphant.

Urgently, Mara smiled and called up to the warriors in Iceni, 'We're friends, not enemies, not Roman!' The girls started to cry.

A spearwoman yelled, not in Iceni, and beckoned. The warriors were Trinovantes. Victoria exchanged a desperate glance with her mother, but what else could they do? Stay there and be speared like fish in a puddle? Pin would only reach the warriors' feet . . .

They handed up the little girls, screaming in terror, 'Mother, Vicky, Mother!' Victoria had to tear their hands away when they tried to hold on to her neck. The men reached down to take Mara's wrists and heave her up. 'Gently, please!' she begged, but they dragged roughly, making her cry out as her leg knocked the side of the well.

Victoria hesitated, but then, ignoring her sprained ankle, hauled herself up the notches in the tree-trunk till she could sit on the edge and swing her feet up.

The girls were suddenly silent; and Mara.

They were lying to one side, beside Bron's body; all dead; one man already tying Mara's long red plait to his belt.

Victoria's heart died in her. Mother . . . O gods . . . Finia – Tilla – No!

Pin was in her hand, she was on her feet. Not expecting this, the warriors leapt back. Under the low ceiling they had little room to swing their long weapons, and she stabbed and slashed, berserk, dancing to dodge their blows, feeling no pain in her bad ankle. In seconds she had driven them back, two wounded in the arms and chest, one on his back with a slashed leg.

She faced Prestia.

The girl's face had turned from gloating to terror. 'No – no!' she screamed, as Bron had done. Pin stabbed forward, almost of its own volition. Victoria felt quite surprised as Prestia's mouth opened in an 'O!' of astonishment. 'Please, no! Not fair!' the girl whimpered, and fell, sliding down off the sword-point in a graceless, whimpering huddle of limbs and torn, dirty dress.

Victoria glared down at her. 'Why?' she demanded. 'Why tell them?'

'Couldn't help it . . . They killed Servic – I was afraid . . . You had everything – why not me – not fair . . .' Prestia's thin voice trailed off.

At a grunt and movement to her left – absently, almost, Victoria held Pin stiff to guard against a sword-swipe that drove the blade back flat against her ribs, started to stab in

140

return. A voice shouted behind her, something hit her elbow, half paralysing her arm.

Her opponent's long sword swung back, ready to cut her in half this time – a cracking pain in her head—

She slid and slid and slid down a whirlpool of swirling lights, into a tiny point of blackness far below.

XI

Cram's voice, somewhere above Victoria, gradually came into focus, began to make sense through her swimming, swirling dizziness. 'I know you can hear me. Listen, Boudicca, it's important. I told the Trinovantes that whatever the girl had said, the fact was that you were my slave, I had sent you to save my aunt and her children. Would they refuse to believe a bard – even an apprentice? Especially when I had stunned you to save one from your blade. Since they already had three heads, one each, they decided to believe me, helped me mount, and slung you across the saddle in front of me. So I brought you away.' Cram sighed. 'Some of it was true. And now the rest, also. For now you must be my slave in truth.'

'Slave?' she muttered. 'Your slave?' What was he talking about? Oh, her head hurt!

Slowly, she understood what he said, where she was, what had happened. Oh, Mother!

She wished she was dead.

'Yes, you must be my slave. You understand me, Boudicca? I can't protect you otherwise.' His dark eyes glanced down at her. 'Also, for your sake I lied, claiming a high rank I do not have, in order to rescue you. You will not damage my honour further by making me even more of a liar.'

He sat on a hillside by the Cheswell ox-wagons, gazing out over the burning town, his face crimson-lit by the flames in the valley below. Beside him, Victoria lay on a blanket – a thick Roman one, loot from somewhere. Around them, she became aware of happy crowds of warriors and their families relaxing and revelling with horns of ale, pointing and cheering as walls crumbled, and roofs crashed, tossing galaxies of sparks high above them among crimson billows of smoke that lit the darkening sky like a hundred sunsets. Soon there would be nothing left of the town but ash.

Victoria didn't care. She had nothing left anyway.

She said it aloud, whispering past the aching bruise across her ribs, right through her heart. 'Nothing left. Everything in my life . . . Mother, my sisters, my friends, Bron, all dead. My home. All gone. My father – Rufius – he betrayed us all. My little brother. Are they still alive? I'll never see them again, anyway. Everybody here hates me. What have I to live for?'

Cram spat in her face.

'What – Why – How dare you?' she gasped.

He snorted in contemptuous amusement. 'Why so angry? If you have nothing to live for, you have nothing to defend – so you cannot be insulted. But you are. You are outraged. So, you still have pride in yourself. And that is what you must live for. Yourself.'

143

Maybe he was right . . . No. It wasn't worth the bother. Her temper sank again.

He studied her a moment, his head cocked to the side as was usual when he was thinking. 'Also for my sake. You will not waste what I did, make me look a liar and a fool. So you have two reasons to live, not to despair and sink.' His voice deepened to the formal tone he had learned from somewhere, that was so impressive: 'The druid Con Veile laid a geas on my father to protect you. He sent me to your home to seek for you, even after you stole his chariot and horses. You will not renege on your debts, to her or him or me. You are not so wretched, nor so disgraced, that death is better than life.'

An irritation drifted through the back of her mind; he spoke as if he was her grandfather. Though he was the same age as Victoria, and smaller, he was much, much older and bigger inside; wiser. Maybe it came from being crippled, with more time to think deeply, instead of running about, exercising.

What did it matter? What did anything matter?

Now, looking down at her, Cram shrugged. 'It will be hard. Mac Clanna will gloat. The whole tribe will despise you, even the slaves – the other slaves. But you will live up to your name. You will not be conquered.'

Her gaze wandered past his thin, intense face bent above her, dark against the burning sky. 'Everything I've done has turned out wrong,' she muttered. 'Even letting that girl Prestia go free when she tried to steal my horses – if I hadn't, she wouldn't have been able to betray mother and Tilla and Finia.'

Cram didn't disagree. 'Fate. Three things come and go in their own time, not as pleases you – a cold in the head, rain, and life. Mara's death you avenged, as you should. You could do no more. Be at peace about that. And for the rest – Con Veile said you were important, but no sign of it have I seen yet. So whatever you have to do is still to come.'

'What?' Her voice was dull, hopeless.

'Ach, how should I know?' He snorted contempt, waving a hand at the whirling red smoke above him. 'Is it an ovate I am, to see the future in the clouds? Wake up, cousin! Make your own future. You can start by mourning your mother my aunt, and your sisters my cousins. A thought I offer you – their death was swift, far better than our women have given many Romans in revenge for what was done to the queen. Not much comfort, but still . . . But still, they died. True. Yet consider also, they would probably have died even if you had not been betrayed, when the house burned over you. All of you. Yes, you alone lived. But you did not kill them, you tried to save them – as I did. We both failed, but that does not make us guilty of their deaths. I feel bad, too, that I could not save you all. However, you I *did* save, which is a small success to take the worst edge off my regret. So, weep for your family, make them a funeral sacrifice, send them on to the Golden Land with your love – but then get on with your own life.' He rose, grimaced in a friendly way, and limped off, his harp swinging on his shoulder.

145

Victoria stared up, unseeing. Her own life . . . What good was that? Tilla's little wooden doll she had loved so much, kicked into a corner beside her body . . . weep for them . . . She finally started to cry.

After a long time, wept out for the moment, she rolled over and pushed herself to her feet. Her ribs, and her ankle, and the old bruise on her stomach, hurt whenever she moved or breathed, but what else was she due, she who had been so useless?

She limped off through the clustering wagons, past the camp fires ringed by rejoicing, singing, dancing tribesfolk, past the crowd and on down towards the brilliant holocaust that spread by now right across the town, roaring and gulping, scarlet flames clawing at the black sky. In the centre of the town the burning houses and shops combined into a seething cauldron of fire; towards the edges the lights were more scattered as warehouses and workshops, sheds and stables blazed, linked by a tracery of smouldering fences. No one heeded her, apparently just another lad among hundreds.

One man was displaying the head of Claudius the God's gilded statue, boasting, 'I've never taken a god's head before!' Others were tossing surplus heads into the nearby stream that ran down to the river, an offering to the local gods. She needed a sacrifice, too – but not a head . . .

While she walked, she drew her eating knife and started

to hack off her hair as close to the scalp as she could, wincing as the blade tugged and crunched through the thick plait.

Pin was no longer at her hip. But then, slaves did not carry swords. She would have to get used to that.

She suddenly realised that she was thinking of the future. Maybe she *hadn't* given up. She wasn't ready to die yet. In spite of all she had lost.

She limped as close as she could bear to the nearest houses, flaring like bonefires. This was the street of big new houses that Dio had drilled the water pipes for. Even twenty paces away, the heat crisped her eyebrows and scorched the skin of her face. 'Mara, my mother, daughter of Cermona, cousin of Prasutaeg, King of the Iceni; Rufinia, Aegyptilla, my sisters, daughters of Mara; I give this to the gods in sorrowful offering for you. In life you were generous and loving, strong and brave. In death, may the Three Mothers, Hera, Vesta, Isis, all the gods receive your spirits kindly.' She limped forward, tossed the long red plait into the blaze, turned—

In a sudden almost-silence in the gusting roar, a voice wailed, 'Boudicca . . .'

A spirit, speaking through the fire? A god?

She made herself face the flames again. 'Who is it? What do you want of me?'

Again the faint, distant scream, louder, more desperate. 'Boudicca . . .'

Grimacing against the heat, shielding her face with a hand, she peered into the flames – past them – and suddenly, thirty strides away, in the narrow street between the burning houses, made out a dark, shapeless figure, waving an arm, trying to crawl, painfully inching forwards. It collapsed to the ground, but still stirred feebly. Someone was caught in the blaze – poor doomed soul! She drew back. It raised a head.

'Help . . . Boudicca . . . Help . . .' It was – no, it couldn't be . . .

'Arvenic? Oh, gods! Somebody help me! Help, here, help!' She waved and beckoned up towards the rollicking crowds above her, but they paid little heed. The few who had noticed her, and wondered at the lad creeping so close to the heat, simply waved cheerfully back.

No time to go up, convince people there was someone alive down here, get them to come down to aid her. She had to go alone, now.

She couldn't! Not deep into the inferno!

She must. She paid her debts, too.

She pulled her boar-hide jerkin up over her head, snatched up a torn cloak lying near her feet, ripped it in halves to wrap round her hands. Two deep breaths with her back towards the fire, where the air was slightly cooler – then she turned and hurried downhill, limping into the furnace.

Afterwards she could recall little except a dazzling roar, and heat blasting all round her. She vaguely remembered falling on her knees beside her uncle, lifting a leather-swathed arm across her shoulders to roll over and haul the heavy body up half on to her back. She tried to rise, but he was too heavy for her bad ankle to support. She had to crawl, scrabbling and struggling, half lifting, half dragging him groaning up the slope between the burning houses.

But of the toppling roof, the beam that half stunned her, the sizzle of her cut hair frizzling under the blazing thatch as the jerkin slid off her head, the agony in her nose and throat and lungs, the red-hot ash under her knees and hands, the terror that she was lost and going the wrong way, the desperate craving to drop Arvenic and run, the stubborn, fierce temper that forced her on, no she'd not give in, never, on and on and on . . . Of all that, she was lucky enough to have no recollection.

When the carousing warriors finally realised the emergency and ran down to help her, she was almost out of range of the heat. Her arms and legs kept on crawling for several seconds after they lifted Arvenic off her back, even after they lifted her to take her to safety.

They carried her behind Arvenic up to the Cheswell wagons, where Aliss received him almost resignedly. 'Lay him in the wagon there! I knew you were hurt, you old fool, when you weren't back for your supper. Your feet, what a mess, were you playing football with a sword?'

'A sickle.' Arvenic's lips twitched. 'Chased old witch into

house, she hit me with sickle. Knocked her down, tripped over it.'

'Teach you not to chase older women!' She bit her lip to hide her worry. One heel tendon was cut right through, he'd never use that foot again, and the sole of the other foot was deeply gashed. 'Warm water, Mor, and my sewing bag. Caluis, run for a druid, Con Veile if you can find her. What's that stench? The old woman's perfume? What have you been doing, swimming in a tanner's pits?'

'Yes.' It was all he could manage, for the moment.

'That's why you're swaddled like a baby in all this stinking leather? Help me get it off, girls. Where's all this blood coming from? Oh, Mothers, look at that slash across his ribs! Mor, a big needle and thread. Lucky you are, sweetheart, a handsbreadth lower and that would have gutted you. Wait till she says yes next time!' Working fast, Aliss washed and stitched the gash.

Meantime, Cram called the other women. 'Fillean, Wenda, come help Boudicca!'

They all drew back, one spitting in disgust. 'She's a traitor!'

'She saved the thane my father!'

'Even so. She's unlucky.' They looked insulted, embarrassed, resentful. One finally found an excuse; 'If the gods have called her spirit, it's not for us to deny her to them.'

'The Three Mothers give you the same kindness that you show her!' Cram spat at them. Nearby a new slave was hovering uncertainly, not understanding Aliss's rapid Iceni. She was a stolid, friendly young woman who had simply walked into their camp outside Camulodunum and started working, and so had saved her life. 'Melissa, aid me!' he called in Latin. Grateful for something she could comprehend, she hurried to help.

Between them, disregarding Victoria's moans, they stripped off the charred remains of the leather jerkin, the tunic and trousers. They gently soaked away the tatters of the cloth wraps on her hands, the scorched leather boots that had saved her feet. With cool water they rinsed off the coated cinders of her hair and the skin beneath.

'Her left hand's burned right through the cloth,' Melissa muttered. 'An' a shockin' gash on her head, an' what a bump! Cracked her skull, likely, an' her hair all burned, never grow back that won't. An' her scalp, an' her poor knees, she'll likely be crippled worse'n—' She glanced nervously at Cram. 'Kinder to let her die.'

Semi-conscious, trying to sink deeper away from the pain, Victoria heard the words, and agreed with them; but, 'No,' a voice said above them. 'She has yet a thing to do in this world, before she crosses the bridge of swords.'

Con Veile stood beside them. She nodded down to Cram. 'I believe your father will recover. He fell in a tannery, badly wounded, left for dead. He woke to see fire all round, sensibly swaddled himself in wet hides against the flames, and crawled away to where the gods sent Boudicca to find him. His hair

151

and moustache are burned off. It's that bothers him most – and the fear that everyone will laugh at him, that it was an old woman who did it!'

She snorted in wry humour, and then sobered. 'Cram, if your father had taken a mail shirt from the Romans at Camulodunum, as many did, his chest would be whole now. Your mother said he spoke of it, but you argued most vehemently against it, it was not traditional.'

Cram bit his lip. 'I said only cowards wore armour. His wounds are honourable!'

'Honourable? Given by an old woman?'

He looked furiously frustrated. 'Am I to blame for them?'

She smiled slightly. 'Partly. Fanatical you were, so righteous, so compelling . . . No father wants to seem less in his son's eyes. But the blame lies not all on your shoulders. He could have refused to listen to you. It was his choice. And even a mail shirt would not have saved his feet.' She shrugged ruefully. 'No one knows what will best please the gods, for even they change their minds! Relax your rigidity a little. Old ways are not always the best. However strongly you feel, you may be wrong.'

She stretched to ease her back, and knelt to take Victoria's hand. 'Boudicca, I know you can hear me. You will be in pain, now and later, but you will keep fighting. You will not give up. Never. Now, drink this poppy juice, it will bring you rest. Drink.'

Half conscious, Victoria swallowed the sour liquid poured into her mouth, and thankfully felt the pain sink into a dark hole away in the distance, nothing really to do with her . . .

Aliss and Con Veile washed Victoria, anointed, stitched, splinted straight the damaged fingers of her left hand so that the burns across the palm and fingers would not pull them into a permanent fist, bandaged, poulticed, prayed constantly. At last, sighing in weariness, they rose.

The druid gave Melissa her sacred silver cup. 'Fetch me fresh water from the spring up there.' Understanding the gesture, the girl trotted off willingly. 'Aliss, let nothing trouble her. Play for her, Cram, soothe her.' She dipped a bunch of her herbs in the water the girl brought back. 'Bouda, goddess of victory, help your namesake now!' She sprinkled Victoria's face and hands, chanting,

'Three drops of cooling water of feverfew – serenity, hope, healing.

Three drops of soft water of willow – ease, suppleness, grace.

Three drops of pure water of valerian – courage, determination, strength.

By the Three Mothers, I call the spirits to nurse you,

Spirits of feverfew, ramson and heart's ease for health,

Spirits of willow, raspberry and vine for agility,

Spirits of valerian, oak and holly for victory.

Three times three is the charm, three times three the blessing.'

153

She tucked the leaves under a flap of bandage and rose, her face stern. 'Boudicca, listen to me from your sleep, hear me in your dreams, take my words into your soul. The gods instruct me to lay this geas on you; you will never surrender, never give up, never abandon your struggle. All through your life, you will fight to the end, for they are with you. Always.'

Cram and Aliss, standing respectfully back, blinked in amazement. A geas was always an inspiration from the gods; now *two* had been laid around Boudicca! But Con Veile shook her head when they would have questioned her, and left without another word.

When Mac Clanna heard that Boudicca had returned, he hurried to see her, grinning in triumph, all ready to gloat and torment his enemy now she was helpless. Aliss stopped him dead, and told him what Victoria had done for Arvenic, and what the druid had ordered; 'She is to rest in peace and calm, without annoyance – and I will see to it!' Glowering, he turned away.

Thoughtfully Aliss watched him go, and exchanged a speaking look with her son. He nodded. 'Can she have the new girl?'

Aliss assented. 'She's willing, but not much use till she learns to speak Iceni.'

'Thank you, Mother.' He spoke to the girl in Latin. 'Melissa, stay with Boudicca, all the time. Especially at night. Sleep by her, in case she wakes, or anyone tries to – disturb her. She might need a drink, or willow bark, or—' he shrugged. 'Or anything.'

Melissa looked after the handsome young warrior, stalking off in frustrated anger to rejoin his friends. She had quickly learned to loathe him, like all the slaves, and she had been disgusted by his expression as he looked at the hurt girl. She nodded. 'Won't nobody nor nothin' bother her, master!'

But she slept soundly, and did not notice the figure that crawled under the wagon beside them that night, to whisper in Victoria's ear.

For sixteen days Victoria tossed in fever and pain. She rose occasionally to a brief wakefulness, enough to drink soup and moan as her wounds were tended, then sank back to insensibility. For a few days Con Veile and Cram sang over her, driving off the worst nightmares. In her sleep, the druid's voice instructed her, 'The gods are with you! You will not give up!' It drove away the horrors when Certinus smiled at her, when she saw again her mother's and sisters' deaths, and the shocked surprise on Prestia's face. She clung to those words when, often and often, in her dreams a handsome face hovered over her, ghastly blue in the moonlight, deep blue eyes gleaming, and a voice muttered, 'I'll get you! Some day, I'll get you! I can wait!'

XII

Like her uncle, Victoria had been fit as a flea. Within four days of recovering full consciousness, after wounds that would have kept a city woman in bed for months, she was hobbling about.

Her head ached all the time, and occasionally she saw double. Her face, swollen for days, slowly worked itself easy again. Her right hand was stiff and painful; the left was worse, the fingers drawing down into a claw over the burns. But she spent hours every day rubbing the frightful scars on her knees and shins with Con Veile's ointment, which helped them all heal and suppled her fingers till her hands opened fully, and her joints began to move freely as they used to.

Aliss soon discovered how Victoria's dreams were haunted by ghosts, for in her nightmares she tossed and cried out, waking half the house. 'I know I saved Certinus, but I still feel bad,' she wept one night, clutching her aunt's hand in distress. 'And I couldn't save my mother, and Rufinia, and little Tilla . . . And that stupid, mean-minded, treacherous girl, she got my mother and sisters killed, after I let her and her lover off! But still . . . Could a druid help me?'

Aliss huffed ruefully. 'We don't have one handy, my dear. But you don't need one, not if you use a bit of common-sense and think!'

Victoria sniffed. 'That's what everybody tells me to do.'

'So try listening to them! Did Certinus want to stay alive? No? Then why would he be haunting you? Your family loved you. Would they ever curse you for not being a god, able to wave a hand and waft them to safety? Of course not! You did all you could. It's your own conscience that's haunting you, my dear. Even with that treacherous girl. If anyone deserved death, she did. Even there, you acted in grief and fury, and also, don't forget, sheer panic, for you expected to die yourself. In any case, the Trinovantes would have killed her themselves, they like traitors no more than anyone else. You shortened her life by no more than minutes. Yes, you feel guilty; but that is because you are a kindly person.'

She chuckled at Victoria's surprise. 'True it is. Killing does not come easy to you. You don't enjoy it. When you do, or when you don't care, that's when your conscience will stop gnawing at you. So, in a way, Boudicca, you can be glad of it, it shows you are human. And like any wound, lass, it will all fade if you don't scratch at it. Give it time.'

Victoria sighed. 'I suppose you're right. But – what do I do meantime?'

'Bear it. What else can you do? For now, drink this milk that Melissa has warmed for you. A good lass she is, her temper honey-sweet as her name. Go back to sleep, my dear. The

157

spirits of your family are happy in the Golden Land. Don't disturb them by this wild sorrow. It recalls them here, to where they suffered. Leave them in peace, and they will leave you in peace.'

She settled her niece down under the blankets again and returned to her own bed, shaking her head. Silly girl. Worse was done every day, with no hint of remorse.

Victoria's hair, all burned off, would never grow properly again. Arvenic, who had been hopping about with a peg-leg and two crutches before she woke, had the same problem. 'Oh, uncle, your fine hair, your glorious moustache!' Victoria mourned some days later, eyeing the half-healed scars wriggling over his head.

He chuckled. 'Ach, the moustache is growing again. And I'll get Aliss to tattoo all over my scalp to cover the scars, red, black and blue. Striking, eh?

'Boudicca could have fun with different wigs,' Aliss suggested.

Victoria sniffed. 'I could have done that anyway! But at least my face is unscarred.' She grimaced. 'Ach, I was never a beauty before, so what matter? But – what do I do now?'

'Well. Since you are thinking of the future . . .' Aliss exchanged wry glances with her husband.

Victoria felt a nervousness; something unpleasant was coming . . .

Arvenic reached up automatically to tug his moustache, and looked peeved as his hand slid off mere bristles. 'While you were wandering in the dream land, Boudicca, Cram and Con Veile went off with the queen's army, after the Romans. Right through Verulamium Suetonius ran; left it undefended like Londinium. Another great slaughter and burning, I hear. However, by now he will have found his army, and the queen must face the legions. A real battle at last! Most of our wounded have recovered and hurried to join her. But three were left, like me, too badly hurt to do battle. They and their families plan to go home. Tomorrow. And,' he grimaced, 'we must go with them.'

He drew a deep breath. 'It's crippled I am, forever. Almost healed the cuts on my chest and my left foot are, but this tendon on my heel will never join, the foot will always flap. A peg-leg, aye, well enough, but . . . Already my people are questioning my authority. Among them I must stay, to remind them that my position as their leader depends on sharpness of wit, and good judgement, as much as strength and agility. If they go home without me, when I do return it's a new thane I may find in Cheswell. I must fight him, or be outcast. I would lose, and die. Cram will become a bard, but marry again Aliss must, probably only as a second or third wife, or become a slave. You see? We must go home.'

'But all the women are agreed, they will not have you back, Boudicca.' Aliss's mouth was tight with indignation. 'The plague they'd prefer. Argued ourselves blue in the face we have, but . . . Can you imagine what life would be like, and we taking you with us? Wildcats in a sack wouldn't be in it!'

'Another problem for my uncle.' Victoria nodded. 'I've brought you nothing but trouble. I'm sorry.'

'Trouble? You saved his life!' Aliss protested. 'But yes, it would cause trouble to insist that you go with us – except as a slave.'

'And that I will not allow, since my life you saved.' Arvenic was definite.

'Well – I owed you, for stealing your chariot and horses—'

'Forget that. I wish everyone repaid their debts so fully! But I fear, Boudicca, you must stay here. Till you are recovered, at least.'

Victoria's head was aching. Alone again . . . But she'd survive. Never give up.

As if he had heard her, Arvenic grinned wryly down at her. 'You will have company for a while. Berrin found some Roman horses straying. A stallion, magnificent as the sun. A broken leg, but he can mend it, he swears, and take it home.' The tall man tutted in admiration. 'Tach, no-one else could hope to do it. But it will not be fit to travel for at least a moon.'

'Melissa can stay, too.' Aliss was brisk to hide her distress. 'She's a good-hearted girl, and willing – too willing! She's been going through the lads like a hot knife through lard. Half

160

a dozen of the women are eyeing her slitty-ways, and two hair-pullings we've had already.'

Victoria made herself smile. 'Don't fret about me. I might even stay here, and rear pigs.'

'You, a pig farmer? Huh!' Aliss snorted disbelief. 'But certainly you must stay here for now. Rest, recover fully. If Cram returns, seeking us, you can tell him where we are. And if the queen is wanting you, we can find you.'

Arvenic hurried to reassure Victoria's alarm. 'Don't worry, she came here while you were ill, and seemed to think you had brought us luck. Aliss just means she may want to talk to you.'

'I don't suppose anyone will claim the land,' Aliss mused. 'Robbers, maybe . . .'

'We'll leave you a couple of dogs. And I have a gift for you. Mog!' Arvenic called a slave boy. 'The long, thin parcel under my bed – quick, now!'

Victoria's face lit up. 'Pin?'

'No, niece. It's lost she is, in your home. Too small for you, in any case. You have grown a handspan since we met, did you not realise? A proper sword you're needing, not a long knife. But I know you prefer the Roman style. So – ah, here's Mog. See what you think of this.'

It was a full-length Roman sword, four inches longer than Pin, with silver wire and carnelian studs decorating the hilt and red leather scabbard. The blade was elegantly inlaid with gold, a tiny scene of a boar-hunt. Speechless with delight, she kissed the beautiful weapon.

Arvenic beamed at her. 'From Italy, I'm told. You like her?'

'Oh, yes! Yes! I'll call her − I'll call her Needle. A larger version of my Pin!'

Aliss burst into laughter. 'Better stitchery you'll do with her than with the usual kind, that's certain! But see what I have for you − I found some lengths of blue-dyed cloth in a chest, and sewed you a new shirt and trousers. And the inside layers of the hides that saved Arvenic I used to make new, soft boots to replace the ones that saved your toes. It's ready for anything you'll be, as soon as you're steady on your feet!'

Next morning, Victoria limped out to see them off with kisses and hugs. As Aliss drove their heavy ox cart up the track, laden with plunder from two towns and several farms, she waved a cheerful farewell and Arvenic called a blessing.

The drivers of the other three wagons and the herd-boys turned their heads away as they passed.

'May the gods send good fortune to you all!' Victoria called. She hoped they felt guilty!

Then she beckoned her companions to sit on the long bench by the door. 'We need to talk. Melissa, pour ale for all of us. Yourself, too.' She poured a few drops for the gods. 'Fortuna and the Three Mothers favour us all, here and everywhere, now and for ever! Now. I plan to stay here, for a while, at least.

It's a good steading, there must have been five or six families living here. This house is solid, good walls and thatch, with a fine big room and plenty of sleeping space in the loft. We'll use the hut next door for a byre, it's got room for Berric's three horses, and we can re-thatch one of the smaller ones for a store when the harvest is ready. The stream's handy for water. We have three apple trees and two pears, and gooseberries. My uncle left us two dogs, the bitch is heavy in pup; a cow and a late calf; two sows with eight piglets and a young boar; and a sack of oatmeal.'

'Goats in the woods, too, I've heard them,' Berrin commented. 'I'll lure them in with windfall apples. And net some geese, when they arrive.'

'There's two broody hens in a bramble patch up the hill, the women missed 'em cos they was quiet, see, an' I kept me gob shut,' Melissa volunteered. She was about five years older than Victoria, pretty, lively and competent. 'Some onions an' beans left. Wild cabbage an' hog-weed by the stream, for the pigs. The field has oats an' barley an' rye growin', the horses an' oxen grazed a lot but there's still some. Ain't great soil, but not bad. An' good trees for firewood an' acorns an' beech mast for the pigs later on.'

'You know more about it than I do. You were a farmer's daughter?' Victoria asked.

Melissa grinned. 'Daughter an' wife, mistress. But me man beat me night an' mornin', said I had a rovin' eye. Not far

163

wrong, neither! No loss he was, not to me, never so well off as wi' you lot. Sorry to see yer lads go, I am. But do yer best wi' what ye've got, I say.' Her eyes slid sideways to Berrin, who looked smug. 'You see to the fields, an' keep off raiders, an' I'll run the house for ye. Ain't no great cook, but—'

'I'll teach you my mother's recipes. Berrin, what about your horses?'

'A crime it would be to leave them, lass,' Berrin said. 'The stallion's the finest I've ever seen, a splendid bright bay, bigger than our horses, from Iberia, I think, and two good mares, left behind because they were sick, but they'll be fit to travel when he is, he'll beat all the others in Cheswell, be king stallion in days—'

Gently Victoria interrupted the flood of enthusiasm. 'Right, fine. What help do you need?'

Cut off in mid-dream, he took a second to bring his mind to what she was saying. 'Er – I have the leg splinted but I'll sleep by him, and if he falls I'll call you to help me get him up. Lucky it's a foreleg, I'll rig a sling—'

'Better call Melissa first – er – till my knees strengthen.' Melissa's eyes were merry, and the corners of her mouth tight to hide a smile. Victoria bit her lip. 'Is he all right now? It must be an hour since you checked on him.' Reminded, he hurried off, while the young women clung to each other in silent glee.

Soon Melissa and Victoria were no longer slave and mistress.

For the first time ever, each found she had someone of an equally tough, intelligent, open mind to talk to and laugh with; someone who understood, who could sympathise and comfort. Both blossomed in their friendship as they worked together round the farm, and talked and talked and talked.

'Yer head hurts, don't it? Tell you what – why don't ye try what I done wi' me man's wallopin's? Cut it off from ye, accept it but put it aside, like. Me, I made a cave inside me head, an' hid away in it. Made the pain nothin' to do wi' me, see, kept it far off, outside. Me own self stayed safe tucked away till the blows stopped, like sittin' out a storm, an' then come out an' rubbed me bruises, an' got on wi' me work. Pretended it were worse'n it was, kept the bully happy.' She shrugged. 'It were either that or just give up an' die, an' I didn't see that as no fun neither.'

'H'mm. I wish I'd learned to do that when Rufius beat me. But I'll try it.'

Melissa giggled. 'You plannin' to get beat regular, then?'

'Of course not! If anybody tried it now, I'd – I'd kill him! But you're right, I get dreadful headaches, and . . .' Victoria grimaced. 'Bad times can come on you any day.'

'Never said a truer word, Vicky. Now crash that axe, eh? No firewood, no supper tonight, an' that'd be bad enough for now.'

For a month they lived in the little farm, while the summer flamed towards its golden peak. Two other little settlements

165

nearby were recolonised by refugees who were guardedly friendly, once they had settled the boundaries of each group's land.

Four men appeared one day, one announcing, 'This is my father's house – this land's mine!'

Victoria faced the tribesman down, one hand on Needle. Behind her, Berrin handled his spear with obvious competence, while Melissa held the leashes of the huge fighting dogs and surreptitiously urged them to bark. 'When the Governor returns, you can come to claim it, with your proof. Until then, clear off!' The men eyed the opposition, decided it wasn't worth it, backed off, and moved into a hamlet across the valley.

Berrin grinned at Victoria. 'He didn't have the hands of a farmer, lass, I think they were just trying to take over a good house and land. No way of telling.'

Melissa agreed. 'We're here now, an' we're stayin'.'

Melissa's cooking did not improve; 'Might be I'm too tired to learn, spendin' so much time in the stable at night, helpin' Berrin wi' the horses,' she suggested impishly.

Victoria's headaches faded slowly. Recalling how she had felt with the poppy drink, she copied that feeling. She stuffed the blinding ache into a big black leather bag, firmly tied the top, and put it away from her. Not exactly what Melissa had suggested, but after some practice it worked quite well. She cooked, exercised, weeded the crops, went hunting. Most of the deer had been killed or driven away, but she hit hares and birds with her sling, and once a wolf. They started to lay in hay and wood for the winter.

Berrin said he was not fully satisfied with his stallion's progress, and he'd stay to help them with the harvest. Melissa smiled.

His many skills were better than gold to them. The ploughing and sowing were all done, but he repaired the burned house for a store, cut wood, taught Victoria to tickle trout and snare the birds that attacked their fields and fruit trees. Though not a warrior like Arvenic, he knew several surprising fighting tricks, and fenced with her while she learned the heft of her new Needle; 'She's finely balanced, light in a thrust but heavy in a blow, marvellous!'

The two giant war-dogs with the great spiked collars kept off wolves, and at night their ferocious baying warned off several bands of robbers. The only group which dared attack quickly fled, leaving a lot of blood and a very chewed arm. The neighbours offered three goslings and two sheep, one with twin lambs, in exchange for a pair of puppies.

One still evening Victoria went for water, leaned over the pool they had dug to make filling the bucket easier and, for the first time since the fire, clearly saw her own reflection. She flinched. Yes, she knew from the feel that her hair was all gone, apart from a few bristly tufts here and there, and her scalp was ridged with scars; but deep down she had never realised how applling she looked. Not being beautiful was one thing; being hideous was quite different.

She returned to the house fighting tears.

'What's wrong, Vicky?' Aliss had left behind the rest of the cloth from Victoria's new clothes, and Melissa was busy stitching herself a new gown in the last of the light, but she was always quick to sense distress. 'Yer hair? Aye, I wondered when ye'd think on it.' She dropped the sewing and set a comforting arm round Victoria's shoulders. 'Why not wear a cloth on yer head, stop folk laughin' at ye?'

'Like a dowdy old married wife? I'd laugh at myself if I did that.' Victoria glared, her pride offended. 'I'll not act embarrassed. I'll – I'll do what Arvenic said he was going to do. Get it all tattooed!'

'Never!' Melissa protested, horrified. 'Ye'll look that savage ye'll scare the dogs!'

'I'll not look ridiculous, though! Terrifying is far, far preferable!'

Victoria trotted three miles to hunt through Londinium's rubble for the brightest pockets of the orange-red ash that was all that was left of the town; soot from a candle made black, and woad or blackberry juice made blue and dark red.

Berrin was skilled at this as at most things about the farm. With his knife he carefully cut out the remaining lumpy pads of bristly skin. 'Now you'll not have to keep shaving it.'

He drew curling patterns all over her head, following or

adapting the lines of scar. Then, over ten days, he used Melissa's needle to prick the lines and patterns, deep enough to draw blood, and rubbed in the dyes, over and over. 'Now keep still. It's less painful over a pad of muscle. Where the skin's as near the bone as this, it hurts.' It did indeed, but the bag trick helped.

Watching, Melissa tutted and laughed till the tears came. 'I'll not have nothin' to do wi' it. Not over her face, leave that clear! Oh, Good Goddess, me sides is achin' wi' laughin'! No, that line's too flat, curve it more out this way . . .'

At last, 'Just this red triangle to darken . . . There. Finished. You've sat well, girl,' Berrin praised Victoria. 'Don't try looking at yourself in the pool yet, it's still all swollen and scabby. But when it settles, you'll be – well, you'll stand out, that's for sure!'

True enough; when he finally let her study her reflection, she was astonished at the colours that swirled over her head. Unusual? Yes. Splendid! And she could still cover it with a wig or headcloth in cold weather, or if she wanted to pass unnoticed.

They were all out harvesting the first of the oats one fine morning, when the dogs started to bay. Needle and Berrin's spear were always close at hand, and Melissa had her sickle; they were wary, but scarcely afraid of a battered old cart and three riders.

Berrin commented, 'No way to treat horses, they're worn out. Odd, the driver's sitting, not kneeling.'

'It's Cram driving, and there's Con Veile!' Joyfully, Victoria ran to welcome them. 'Cram! How are you? How's your hand? What are you staring at – oh, my head? Ach, I had to do something when all my hair was burned off. Be welcome, Con Veile, and you warriors!' Con Veile lifted a weary hand in greeting. The two men, one old, one very young, neither Iceni, would not meet her eye. 'You look tired, Cram.' In fact, he looked exhausted. 'Your parents aren't here, they've gone home to Cheswell, did you come looking for them?'

Wordlessly the young man shook his head, and drew back a cloth from what Victoria had thought was a big bundle at his side.

Huddled in a red checked cloak on the cart floor, a woman coughed weakly. Red gold round her neck echoed the red of her matted hair.

Victoria looked back up at Cram. 'Boudicca? Queen Boudicca? What's wrong? Why – what's she doing here?'

It was Con Veile, dismounting stiffly, her face old and craggy as a cliff, who answered her. 'She insisted we come to find you, girl. She is dying.'

XIII

The two warriors rode on; 'She is not our queen. We've done what we can.'

Slant-mouthed with scorn, Berrin unharnessed the staggering ponies from the cart, led them off to the stream to drink, and then hobbled them in a quiet, sheltered patch of good grass near the house where the poor beasts could feed and rest. Melissa helped Con Veile carry the queen into the house to tend her, while Victoria half carried Cram to the bench by the door.

She brought ale for him. 'Now, what's happened, Cram?' He slumped, avoiding her eye, refusing to speak. 'Tell me!' She shook his arm. 'Tell me, cousin!' Gods, it must be bad!

He drank without looking up. 'The rebellion is broken. The tribes are destroyed.'

'Destroyed?' Her breath caught. 'You mean – completely?'

A shoulder shrugged. 'A few still live. But . . . the queen, and the druids, and all of us who wanted to fight Rome, we have led our people to ruin.' Abruptly, he forced himself to his feet, to stare out over the fields.

'Even if the Romans won a battle—'

Cram snorted. 'Won a battle?' He sobbed, deep in his throat, and mastered himself. 'Listen then. I'll tell you.' She offered his harp; she had carried the bag in and laid it on the bench, but he shook his head. 'No . . . Maybe never again . . . Ach, well.

'We chased the Romans to Verulamium and burned that town, like Camulodunum and Londinium. And still the Romans fled, north and west. More tribes joined rejoicing in our victory.' The chanting cadences of the bard were in his voice; even in his torment, as they travelled he had been starting unconsciously to form a song.

'As they fled, so we followed, to and fro through the hills, until at last in a steep-sided valley we trapped them, two tired legions against our hundred thousand triumphant warriors.

'Our women drove up the wagons to watch, packed tight into every space around.

'The Romans stood in long, thin lines across the valley. Eight or nine lines. We laughed, they were so few, and all small men, a head less than our warriors. We would stroll over them! Our heroes dashed out, swift and dazzling as kingfishers with their golden torcs and armlets, gleaming helmets and shields, fine chariots and spirited horses, tossing their swords high to flash in the sunlight, challenging the Romans to fight, their champions against ours. They did not accept the venture. They sat down! They sat and watched, while we all jeered at their silent fear.

'At last the chariots were drawn aside, into the woods at the sides of the valley, out of the way, and Boudicca gave the signal

172

to charge. Forward our warriors raced, screaming the battle-cry, brandishing their mighty swords, irresistible as the storm. The women howled and cheered them on.

'The Romans did not panic and flee. A horn blew. They stood up, and gave a single shout, and prepared to receive the charge.

'Each man had two javelins. The front rank threw, then the second, and then the third. Then again. Six flights of javelins, like hail slashing down the valley. The small, sharp spear-points pierced our warriors' shields, through to the hearts behind. Our second and third ranks stumbled over a pile of killed or wounded.

'Still, we had twenty times as many men, and we were free heroes, noble warriors, not paid servants of the tyrants.

'But the Romans locked their shields high, overlapping, a wall of shields facing us, and the middle ranks locked shields behind them, to brace their backs. We could not thrust them back, and as the warriors behind pushed forward, we were jammed till we could not move our arms, our spears and long swords. The pack was so tight the dead could not even fall. The Romans, though, stabbed through between their shields, or underneath.'

'I told Arvenic short blades were deadly at close quarters.' Victoria's voice was faint with grief and horror.

'At last, our men drew back away from the crush and dust, to breathe.

'The Romans did not draw back. The shields turned sideways, and the middle rows marched forward between them, through their weary front ranks, to face us fresh and untouched, trampling on our men's bodies.

'We charged again. A second time, the javelins, and the stabbing underneath among the packed warriors, while now their front ranks rested in the rear.

'The war-horns called our men back again, to admit others in their turn. As they withdrew, again the rear Roman lines slipped through their shield wall – but this time they kept on marching. They tramped steadily on towards us, that row of shields, like the tide coming in, relentless, forward and forward, the other lines close behind them now. If one fell, instantly another filled his place. Unkillable they seemed, eternally renewed.

'The Romans in the rear rank plucked javelins from the corpses, and threw them over the heads of their own men. One struck the queen where she stood on her chariot, urging on her warriors – yes, we were packed that tight and close. A man who saw it turned to run, another, then all. But by this time they had backed against the wagons, among the oxen and carts and children screaming now in fear, not triumph. The sides were blocked by the parked chariots. And the Romans still coming and coming . . .

'Hand to hand over the heads of the women Boudicca was handed out over the wagons, calling out to stay and die with her warriors. A druid physician drew out the spear-point and bandaged the wound, but told Con Veile to ride away with her. "Too too old I am to travel with you, it's hold you back I would," he said, and turned to die with the tribes.

The only chariot we could find was that farmer's cart, with poor old nags, despised and left at the rear, too shabby to shine among the glory of our champions. But they were all dead by then, or else wriggling out between the wheels and fleeing, while the women jeered at them and struck at the Romans with ox-goads and axes when they could not turn the jammed wagons. A few carts at the back may have escaped, and some men over the valley sides. Dead are the rest by now, or enslaved, all the warriors and mothers and children of six tribes . . .

'So a cripple, and a druid, and two fleeing cowards are the heroes who carried the queen to safety. East towards home we headed, but Boudicca declared that she would, she *must* speak with you, so we turned south to seek you. Weaker each day she grew, but each day more determined.'

Victoria's lungs felt filled with mud. 'But – did she say why?'

He nodded to Con Veile, coming out of the house. 'Maybe she can tell you.'

Con Veile's face was sombre. 'Go in to her, Boudicca. Speak softly. She has stayed alive only to meet you.'

'Why?'

'I know only what I told you; you still have a thing to do. The gates are opening for the queen, she can see the other side. Maybe she can see what the gods have in store for you. Cram, play for her, ease her passing.'

Victoria's scalp crawled. As she went in she thrust down a sudden nervous urge to giggle; her hair wanted to stand on end, but she hadn't any hair left.

Boudicca was lying on a straw mattress on the bench by the fire, her face and hands washed, her hair tidied, her sunken eyes black-shadowed and her mouth tight against pain. Melissa, holding the queen's head to let her drink, laid her down gently, set down Con Veile's silver cup and slipped out to leave them alone. Outside, Cram's harp sang quietly.

Victoria knelt beside the bed. 'Great lady, what do you want with me?'

The queen's rich voice had faded to a frail breath. 'Romans killed, enslaved us. Then, you came to us . . . Boudicca . . . Victory . . . We fought back. Killed them. Balance tipped even. But you left. Bouda turned from us.'

'You took Verulamium.'

Boudicca hissed in scorn. 'Not triumph. Butchery. Many joined us, but . . . Not noble warriors. Weaklings, who had knelt willingly to Rome. Seeking easy plunder . . . Then . . .'

She drew a tearing breath, and coughed. Blood trickled from the corner of her mouth. She groped for Victoria's wrist. 'You left us. Now – now we are destroyed.'

'It wasn't my fault!' Victoria protested. That was unfair. She felt sick.

'No . . . no. But still . . . While you were with us, we triumphed . . . Now again balance will tilt, till Roman weight throws ours right off the beam. Revenge . . . In a year, not one of my people in three still free. Not one hut in nine unburned. Not one child at all will not know hunger, fear, cold. Slavery best they can expect, slaves are worth silver . . .' Her voice slurred and failed. She paused to gather her forces, with bitter determination.

'You're one of us. I know . . . You'll not allow . . .' Suddenly the dying woman's hand gripped tight with the last of her strength. 'I lay it on you, a geas from a queen; you will punish Rome, the Romans who . . . Balance. As they show mercy, so you . . . But . . . As ruthlessly as they destroy my people, your people, so you will destroy them.'

'Destroy the Romans? Me? But – I'm only one – how can I . . . ?'

The queen's shoulder twitched in a tiny shrug. She coughed again. 'I don't know. But you will. Geas. Must obey . . . victory . . .' The queen's hand fell away. 'Druid. Now.'

Almost unable to breathe, Victoria called in Con Veile. The druid was waiting to hurry in, to kneel in her turn by the queen's side and catch the faint murmur. Victoria could just make it out. 'Lughnasadh – soon? Yesterday? Near enough. Lugh will forgive us . . .' A bout of bloody coughing. 'I go consenting.'

Victoria escaped outside, and leaned against the door-post in shock.

Berrin, coming out of the stable, asked, 'What is it? Is she – dead?'

'No. Not yet. Not quite. But . . .' Victoria paused in anguish, to try to clear her mind. 'She says I've to destroy Rome. She laid it on me as a geas. Me!' They stared in amazement. Cram's hands stilled on his harp. 'Ridiculous! Crazy! And she – she says it's Lughnasadh, the autumn festival, and she wants to go to the god as a sacrifice! Who ever heard of – she's mad! Magnificent, but raving mad!'

'A queen she is, cousin, and the descendant of gods. Do you expect her to be ordinary?' Cram snorted contempt, and started to play again.

Inside the house, Con Veile's voice rose, chanting. They waited; and presently she came out to them. 'She is gone from us. Now we must bury her fittingly.'

Con Veile picked a place two hundred paces from the house, where a little clear hill rose between the stream and the forest. 'Dig a grave here. Not a pyre. A queen is laid to rest in the earth, with offerings to do her honour.' She helped for a while, and then walked off down by the stream. 'I must prepare my mind to call to the god, and gather flowers to line the grave.'

'Offerings.' Shoulder-deep in the hole, Victoria eased her left hand, cramped and aching with spading up the earth that

Cram loosened with a deer-horn pick. 'You know more than me, Cram, what kind of offerings?'

'Food and drink, of course, the best we have; but she should also have a chariot and horses, and dogs, and servants.'

Victoria reached up to pat secure the pile of earth above the grave. 'Well, Melissa is roasting a hare – we can give the queen some of that, it's a sacred beast. And ale. She can have one of the dogs – not the bitch, she's still feeding her pups, but the male. He's fiercer anyway.'

Berrin started to widen the hole. 'That old chariot – I'd not insult her by sending that with her. But –' his jaw clenched '– she can have a horse. The finest horse, for the greatest queen.'

'Berrin! Not your stallion, that you've spent so long nursing? Oh, Berrin!'

'Ach. Both the mares are in foal to him.' The little man smiled darkly. 'For Lughnasadh the sacrifice should in any case be stallion. It is fitting. Let him proudly bear a queen among the flowers of the Golden Land.'

'And the attendant is easy.' Cram's eyes were on Melissa, walking towards them with a jug of ale.

Victoria's heart nearly stopped. 'No! Melissa is my friend.'

Berrin straightened, his face twisted with bitter resignation. 'So? I love the girl, too, but Boudicca is our queen. She is due the best we can give. No mean sacrifice, but something of value!'

'Not my friend!'

Sensing trouble, Melissa stopped. 'What's wrong?'

Berrin moved towards her.

'No!' Victoria snapped.

'What will you do?' Cram glared, his nose nearly touching hers. 'Will you kill us both, to save this Roman girl?' By now Melissa had learned a fair bit of Iceni language, and understood what he said. She gasped, suddenly seeing her danger, as he snarled, 'The queen must have a servant!'

'Not this one!' Victoria scrambled on to the grass, snatched out her sword and jumped in front of Melissa. 'You'll not touch her!'

'If I must, you must,' Berrin hefted his long-handled spade. It was a good weapon, longer than Needle, but she was used to fighting men with longer weapons than her own, and she knew his tricks now—

'What is it?' Con Veile was running towards them. 'What are you fighting about?'

Cram clambered out of the hole. 'Boudicca here – no, call her Victoria, she's not fit to bear that name! She is denying Queen Boudicca this slave girl as a servant in the Golden Land.' White with fury, he threw all the grief and despair of the last days on to Victoria. 'Vile, traitorous, greedy bitch!'

'No more a traitor than you, Cram.' Victoria's hand and voice were both wavering, with rage and her own grief. 'You'll not get my friend as a sacrifice. I killed Certinus to save him from your torture; I'll not let you kill her!' The glint of gold on

180

her sword caught her eye, and stopped her. 'I do honour her, though, and I'll prove it. I will make an offering. I'll give the queen my sword, rather than my friend!' Although that would almost break her heart, it would be better than killing Melissa – or her other friend, her cousin.

Cram's teeth were bared in a grimace of rage. He limped forward, bare-handed. 'Your sword is not a servant! If you want to stop me, you must kill me.'

'I will if I have to! Your choice!'

'You fool, I choose her!'

Berrin grabbed Melissa's arm. The ale jug crashed on to his head, knocking him to his knees. 'Try askin' my choice!' she yelled, leaping to snatch up his spear. 'Think I'll stand still to be slaughtered like a sheep?'

Suddenly Con Veile was in the centre of the group, her tone commanding. 'Stop! Equally fools, the lot of you! Cram, Berrin, you know the sacrifice must go consenting! Roman this girl is, not one of us. She would never serve the queen in the Land of Youth, her spirit would cause nothing but trouble. Like your sword, Boudicca. How could an Iceni queen ever rest at peace with either beside her? In any case, you know neither of you would ever harm the other.' She glared at them till they nodded reluctantly.

Her face was shining; weary, haggard and yet exalted. 'Yes, the queen needs an attendant. And there is one here who will go with her, willingly.' They knew who she meant.

'Now, hurry and finish that hole. An offering to the god of light must be finished in sunlight, and on the day of the sacrifice.'

Silent, resentful, angry, they returned to their digging. Melissa, with a look of pure gratitude at Victoria, ran back down towards the house. Con Veile shook her head at them and went off for another armful of meadowsweet.

XIV

Once assured of her safety, Melissa put on her new blue gown in honour of the occasion. She stood at a respectful, curious distance to attend the queen's funeral, expecting a long ceremony, but finding it remarkably simple and quick.

While Cram played his harp, sullenly avoiding Victoria's eyes, Con Veile and Berrin carried out the queen's body wrapped in her war-cloak, the great golden torc gleaming round her neck. They laid her on a carpet of flowers and sweet herbs, her spear beside her, her mirror in her hand. Victoria handed down their offerings; food and drink, the first corn and apples.

Con Veile prayed;

'Weep, weep, people of the earth, for a great woman is gone from you!

A queen, descended from the gods, goes to join her forefathers,

Leaves us mourning, to journey to the Land of Youth.

Lugh of the light, Lugh of the sky, Lugh of the free air,

Welcome this free spirit into the Golden Land.

Guide her across the stony moor, lead her over the bridge of swords,

Open the gates wide for her to enter and rejoice among the
heroes,

The blessed kings and thanes and warriors,

To sing and feast, dance and do glorious battle forever.

Free she lived, free she died, freely she comes to you.

Honour her as we do, inspire us with her honour,

Praise her as we do, inspire us with her courage.

Accept her sacrifice, accept our sacrifice,

Lift our spirits high and noble, unconquerable as hers.'

Victoria led forward the big dog. Dosed with poppy, he
walked willingly down the ramp. When Con Veile slid her
sharp, slender flint knife into his neck, he yelped only slightly,
before licking her hand and curling up as if to sleep.

The bright bay stallion followed a handful of oats down into
the pit. It snuffed curiously at the flowers, and the dog. Berrin
patted its neck in regret. 'Will I do it, druid? No?' He could not
hide his relief as he climbed out and offered the axe to Con
Veile. 'On the edge above you should stand. Down there, if he
struggles you could be hurt.'

She was absolutely serene. 'Never fear, Berrin. All will go
well this day.'

The horse's head tossed up at the thud of the big axe. It
lifted for an instant on to its hind legs, then folded neatly, laid
its head peacefully down and collapsed gently on to its side. It
kicked three times. Its hooves dug into the wall of the grave,
and an avalanche of the steep-piled soil pattered down, knee-

deep, covering and hiding the bodies at the bottom.

'Tach!' Con Veile exclaimed ruefully as she handed Berrin the axe and lifted her feet out of the earth, shaking the dirt off the skirt of her gown. 'No, do not bother clearing it out. I can lie above them as well as beside them.' She smiled up at them. 'Never mourn me. What is there for me in this world, but to be hunted by the Romans, and in the end die on a cross like any criminal?'

'You are still needed! There are so few druids left. You can heal people, help them see the future, or teach them your skills,' Victoria urged. 'You told me never to give in. You should do the same. Why despair? Maybe I'll manage what the queen told me, and destroy Rome!'

Cram sneered. 'You? Hah!'

'Hush, Cram.' Con Veile laughed quietly as Victoria bristled. 'She will do what she can, and that will be more than anyone might dream. But the sun is low, and before it sets the first stone of the queen's cairn must be laid. Time it is for me to pass on.' She reached for the flint knife which she had laid on the edge of the grave.

Melissa yelled. 'Hey, who're you? Look out!'

A pony that had walked silently through the trees behind them suddenly hurtled forward, knocking Berrin into the grave on top of Con Veile. From its back, a dark figure leapt at Victoria with a triumphant scream. 'Got you, traitor!'

Mac Clanna.

His sword swung hard for Victoria's neck.

Grabbing for Needle, she ducked, almost too late. The blade cracked across the back of her head, just where the falling beam had struck so recently. It knocked her to her knees. A blinding agony filled her skull, paralysed her. Dimly she saw Mac Clanna, his face full of venomous joy, raising his sword again. She couldn't rise, couldn't move . . .

A slight figure shouted, 'No!' Cram. Even though he was angry with her. He grabbed Mac Clanna's arm and tugged, pulling him aside. The bigger, stronger man whipped his blade up. Cram raised his arms, holding Larksong. A melodious crunch. The sword carved through the harp, through both pillars, and on down the side of Cram's head into his shoulder. He screamed.

Somehow that snapped Victoria to movement again. Dizzy, blood pouring down her neck, she drew her sword and shoved herself to her feet. Two or three of him . . . no matter, she had two or three Needles. Ignore the pain in head and knees. Dive in close, inside the swing of his long blade, and stab – yes, it worked, he jumped back. Follow him, don't let the boar off the spear—

Berrin was scrambling out of the grave with the axe. 'Keep off!' she yelled in insulted fury. 'All of you! He hurt Cram! He's mine!'

Berrin hesitated. Grabbing his arm, Con Veile cried, 'Yes, leave them! This is the god's work!'

'I knew if I followed Cram I'd find you! Traitor, doom-bringer! Roman!' Mac Clanna's voice was hoarse with fatigue and hatred.

Victoria drove forward, shrieking in pain and temper, thrusting and stabbing, forcing Mac Clanna back. Her head was spinning. Her neck and elbows kept wanting to melt. Couldn't keep going for long . . .

He had a mail shirt. Not traditional. Not fair . . .

Somewhere out there, Con Veile was chanting . . .

As Victoria dodged a swing a stone turned under her bare foot, her bad ankle twisted and she fell. Her elbow hit the ground. With a sense of outrage, not fear, she watched Needle fly right across the grave, far out of reach. Curse the faithless gods!

Mac Clanna's sword was sweeping down towards her.

She jack-knifed to one side and, as it struck deep into the earth beside her head, her hand touched a stick in the grass. Desperately she grabbed it, and kicked out at Mac Clanna's knees while he was heaving the heavy sword up again. He staggered, his foot slipping slightly over the edge of the grave. While he was unbalanced she kicked again, knocking his leg out from under him, and he started to fall on top of her. She rose on one elbow, thrust the stick up, it was all she had—

It was Con Veile's flint knife. In utter disbelief she watched the narrow, razor-sharp tip slip through a three-link hole in

Mac Clanna's mail shirt, pierce through his tunic, into his chest.

He crashed on top of her fist, driving the knife further in, whined in pain, and tried to rise, straddling her, astonished, his blue eyes wide and brilliant, his mouth open. So confident of winning, certain of killing her, sure of his might, invulnerable in his armour . . . But Lugh had decided otherwise.

Mac Clanna turned sideways, pulled out the knife with a gasp. A gush of blood followed it. He coughed, and then collapsed, crushing her. She shoved in horrified disgust at his shoulders. He slithered slowly off, over the rim into the grave.

'The queen is royally attended,' Con Veile proclaimed. She towered above them, hands raised towards the sinking sun. 'Willingly Mac Clanna, a brave young warrior of Boudicca's own clan, came here and died by the sacred knife. Lugh of the light, accept the sacrifice you have chosen!' She began to chant, falling into her god-trance.

Melissa, impressed but keen to hide it, hurried forward. 'Are ye hurt bad, Vicky? Sit up, lass. He hit yer head again, what a blood pourin' out, can ye see straight? Can ye stand? Gods, would ye look at the state o' ye!'

Berrin was supporting Cram, who sat holding his arm, head twisted to the side, clearly in pain. Swaying, Victoria blinked at him. 'Cram, you saved me. Again. And lost your lovely harp. Nearly lost your arm. After we argued . . . Why?'

Cautious not to move his head, he glanced up. 'I didn't stop to think. Stupid. But even if I had – I suppose . . . I'd have done the same.' He sighed, wincing, pressing the hem of his shirt to his shoulder. 'You are my family, my cousin. My friend, in spite of . . . You would defend her, your friend, I could do no less.'

Con Veile stopped singing. Berrin called her, 'Druid, Cram's collar bone is broken.'

Her prayers finished, she returned to this world, calmly practical again. 'I'll set it. Melissa, take Boudicca down to the house and stitch that cut on her head.' She chuckled in some surprise. 'It seems that I am meant to live after all.'

'Maybe the gods have work for you as well,' Victoria suggested. She grinned hazily down at Cram. At all three Crams. 'The queen got another offering. Your harp, your lovely Larksong . . .' She screwed up her eyes and peered closer. Blood was dribbling down the side of his head. 'You've lost an ear, did you know? Ach, they always stuck out too much. You look less like an amphora now. More like a jug.'

Cram stuck his tongue out at her. 'Will I ask Con Veile to trim the other one, so both sides match?' They were all chuckling, in light-headed relief despite their pain.

'Stop wastin' time. Come on, Vicky, ye look – ye look grisly!' Scolding, Melissa helped Victoria to wobble down the hill. 'That's right, throw up here, not in the house. Now let me slip yer tunic off, an' yer trousers, they're near as bad, I never seen so much blood. Sit down there, Vicky, an' don't you dare faint on me, hear me? I'll put yer clothes in a bucket to soak, steep the blood out.'

In only ten minutes Victoria was stripped, washed and her scalp stitched. 'That'll do. Won't spoil yer precious tattoos too much, shouldn't think. Can sew even if I can't cook.' Melissa hesitated, bandaging cloth scraps round Victoria's head. 'I never thanked ye for standin' up for me. When that twisted little – er – Cram wanted to kill me. Ready to fight for me ye was an' him yer cousin an' all. I'm – I'm grateful.' She pulled off her dress. 'Here, slip this on. Short on ye, but better'n nothin'. Ye'll just have to put up wi' Roman style, look near respectable for once. I'll wear me old one.'

Shakily, Victoria pulled the blue gown over her head, wincing, waving a hand in dismissal. 'No – no thanks needed. You're my friend.' She drew a breath and reached for Melissa's hand. 'Help me up. I must go and help cover the queen.'

'Don't be daft! Three o' them out there, an' two not hurt. They'll manage!'

'I must!' In the end Melissa shrugged and helped her out.

Con Veile was tying Cram's elbow tight to his side over a thick pad of cloth in his armpit. 'That will hold the collar-bone in the right place. Now take care of it!'

The girls stood looking down at Cram's shattered harp laid reverently near the queen's head. Berrin had hauled Mac Clanna's body to curl crouching by Boudicca's feet, in a corner of the grave, his sword clasped in his hands. The little man

190

glanced at Victoria. 'He tried to kill you from behind,' he murmured. 'Shameful. I'd not leave him here – he's not fit to serve the queen. But the druid seems happy, so it must be what the gods wanted. No disgrace to you for killing such a coward, no need for you to feel dishonoured.'

'Dishonoured?' Victoria considered dully for a moment. Her emotions seemed to be as worn-out as she was – or maybe it was just her headache that made everything seem far-off, blurred. 'I don't feel. . . . I don't really care.' He was shocked at her lack of proper pride. She grinned faintly. 'I think Cram was right, I'm not a real warrior. I don't feel guilty, either. He attacked me first. And last year – only last year! So much has happened since – there was a little slave boy, and my boar spear . . . No, it's past, it doesn't matter, just suspicions . . . All I can think of is that he's been in my nightmares ever since the fire. Now he'll not come again. Anyway, he wasn't a coward, just not honourable. Maybe I brought out the worst in him.'

'Plenty o' worst to bring out!' Melissa growled. 'Not your doin', nohow. Don't be soft! Well – you goin' to fill that hole in or leave it lyin' there?'

Berrin clambered to the top of the pile of earth and started to shovel it down, but Mac Clanna's body was still uncovered when hooves thudded quietly below them. 'Horses got out? Gods, what a day!' Berrin growled, swung round – and froze.

A dozen Roman cavalrymen were trotting past the house and up the hill towards them.

191

Victoria felt even more faint. Death for all of them, if the Romans realised they were from Boudicca's army, or even if they decided to kill them and take the horses and pigs. She could see a little herd already being driven away over to the west, where smoke from a neighbour's burning roof showed what could so easily happen at any sign of disloyalty to Rome. Death especially for Con Veile, if she was recognised as a druid. Death for the warrior, Berrin, and the bard, Cram, and the turncoat, Victoria . . .

The only one who might be safe was Melissa. Who had seen her family killed by the Iceni. Who had been given to Victoria as a slave. Who could make herself famous, and probably rich, if she told the soldiers that this was where the great Queen Boudicca's body lay.

What would she do? What would she say?

XV

Berrin was poised to grab the axe again, but Melissa moved first. She danced forward to take the troop leader's rein and grin up at him, scolding cheerfully. 'At last! Who're you lot – Fourteenth Gemina? Took yer time, didn't ye? Could've done wi' ye a while back, wi' that savage tryin' to kill us all, but we managed. He were the first we've seen in a month, it's quiet enough round here now. But still, a sight for sore eyes you are, boys! Come along down to the house an' give us all the news! I got some good ale – can't cook, but by Jupiter, I can brew!'

The decurion in charge blinked in pleased surprise at her enthusiasm. 'Savage? We saw a fight, it looked like, from the hillside over there. What happened? Who are you?'

At least he wasn't ordering them killed. Not immediately.

'Me name's Melissa. Me man were Arrius, veteran o' the Twentieth, he farmed up by Camulodunum. Them stinkin' Iceni took me as a slave, it helps bein' the best-lookin' girl this side o' the narrow seas, eh?' She preened as one rider whistled appreciation. 'I hid away when the hairy beggars headed north.' Her robust good humour and country accent were making an impression. The troopers were still wary but relaxing, sitting

193

back, easing their helmets, resting their spears across their saddles, some starting to smile.

Melissa gestured round to where the others stood trying to look inoffensive and friendly. 'This is me friend, Victoria, daughter o' Rufius Aegyptus, a merchant o' Londinium.' She smiled reassuringly at Victoria, who sighed in relief. She should have trusted her friend.

One of the troop called, 'I met Aegyptus, sir. Two years back. Right enough, he had a big daughter called Victoria. Veteran, sir, from the Second Augusta.'

The faces above her changed to contempt. The troop leader spat. 'That for the Second! Never moved out of their fort in Isca, sat safe on their fat rumps while the rest of us fought the horse queen. Their commander, Poenius Postumus, he's fallen on his sword in shame – no loss; cursed coward! Don't talk to me about the Second!'

Victoria forced herself to nod, though her head felt as if it was falling off. Stuff the pain into a black bag and tie it up tight and you can go on. 'My father would agree with you, decurion. That's just what he said. He despised Postumus, said he wasn't half the man Vespasian had been.' One or two heads nodded. 'I don't know where Father is now, or my baby brother. They disappeared in the fighting.' She swallowed. 'But my mother and my two little sisters are dead. Their heads were taken by Trinovantes.' So hard to say.

They must have seen the truth in her face. Their expressions changed again, to a rough sympathy. 'We'll avenge them lass!' She nodded; that was what she was afraid of . . . 'You were a slave too, Victoria?'

'For a while. Then I was ill and they left me behind.' True, as far as it went. 'Melissa nursed me, and that old woman there.' She pointed to Con Veile. 'She just turned up, worn out and starving. She's half deaf, and half daft, but she can scare birds off the fields at least, and she doesn't eat much.' Behind the men, despite the danger, Con Veile's lips twitched. 'Melissa and I took over this farm, nobody could argue, the people were all dead. That man brought some goats out of the woods and joined us, he's slow, but helpful. And the boy. We took him in, too.'

'As a slave?' The leader seemed to be believing her. If she didn't make any mistakes . . .

'Well, I didn't actually buy him – no officials round about to pay the sale tax to!' That made them laugh. It helped that Cram looked so small and young and helpless. She didn't dare look at him. He had saved her by claiming she was his slave. Ironic, that she was doing the same for him now.

One of the horses had sidled to where its rider could see into the grave. 'Who's that with the war paint? The savage you had trouble with?'

Melissa chuckled. 'Aye. There were another lass wi' us here, see, but she were bad hurt. She died, so we come up here to bury her – an' then this dirty great painted brute rode up an'

195

tried to kill us all! But Victoria there, she nipped his candle for him! You said you seen it?'

'Some of it, too far off to make out details.' The decurion eyed Victoria with respect. 'You killed him? Not your slaves?'

She gestured at Cram's sling and blood-covered head. 'They tried to help, but yes, it was me. And luck.' And more luck, that her head had been hurt so the bandages covered the tattoos; how could she ever have explained them to Roman soldiers? Melissa's gown that she was wearing now was the same blue cloth as her tunic, shortish, but Roman in style; since they had only seen her from a distance, they'd not know the difference, it would satisfy them. And Berrin had laid Needle in her scabbard, beside the grave, not strapped to her waist.

Even as she thought it, one of the cavalrymen dismounted and lifted the scabbard, sliding the sword out till the gold inlay glowed in the sunset. He whistled. 'Quality, eh? This his, miss?'

Miss. Respect. He accepted her story.

'Mine now, trooper.' If he didn't loot it from her.

He only chuckled, slipped it back into the scabbard and handed it to her. 'He could've got it from – well, just about anywhere. But the owner won't be needing it. I'd say you won it, you got a right to it. Right, sir?'

To her relief the decurion nodded, and the men gave her a cheer. Decent young men, all of them, Victoria thought, not vicious or greedy for goods or revenge. They could have been;

she dreaded to think what could have happened. Thank all the gods, they had been so lucky!

He looked round again, more appreciative than predatory. 'Not a bad place you've got here, girls. You won it too, I'd say. We'll see you keep it.'

'Thanks, sir! Knew we could rely on the legions!' Melissa sparkled up at him, and turned to Victoria. 'You get the grave filled in, Vicky. Just leave the savage, Bella were always a wild one, she'd like a bit comp'ny, eh? You, Convia, hurry down and get out every cup an' bowl we got.' Con Veile winked at Victoria and scurried ahead of them, trying to look as small and old as possible. 'Right, lads! Ale!' Melissa beamed at the men. 'An' ye can tell us what's been happenin'. We ain't had word for two month, not since the tribes went north. You beat that Boo-ticker bitch? Praise all the gods! I'll sacrifice a goat to the Good Goddess!' She pointed to where Berrin had tethered Mac Clanna's tired pony. 'Look, there's that thief's pony, take it back wi' ye. Come on, boys, let's celebrate!'

The decurion nodded. 'Just a quick sup, we can't stay long, got to get back and report this area's clear of rebels. You four, give them a hand to fill in the grave, and then come down.'

Melissa was hoisted to the saddle in front of him, squealing, 'Oh, ye naughty devil! Stop that! D'ye treat every girl this way? I'm a decent lass, I am! Put me down at once, ye hear?' in vivacious mock-alarm. As they rode off down the hill, laughing, she peeked round his back and triumphantly waggled her fingers.

Rather suddenly, as her knees folded, Victoria sat down beside Cram. Berrin hovered a moment, but she waved him away. 'I'll be all right. Get on with filling in the grave, don't leave it all to the army the way you left the fighting to me.' She almost laughed at the glare of reproach that he shot at her before getting to work alongside the soldiers.

Cram sat silent beside her.

The sunset, the noises of the evening, and the men's voices, all blurred, swooped round and round her brain. Please, Three Mothers, let her not be falling delirious again!

Gradually, as she sat still, her eyes cleared and her head settled back to a bearable dull ache. When the men had piled most of the earth back over the hole, she could even joke, 'There's always more comes out of a hole than will go back, isn't there?' Especially if you had half filled the hole with bodies, and a horse . . . The soldiers laughed. 'Better hurry down, or the ale will all be gone!' That cleared them off.

Berrin shouldered the spade. 'I'll see they don't steal my horses,' he muttered.

'If they want to take the horses, or anything else, you let them!' she snarled. 'If Melissa can't talk them out of it nobody can. Just be glad you're not wearing a torc. They think you're from a friendly tribe, and don't you dare let them suspect anything else!' He grimaced, but nodded reluctantly. 'But before you go . . . Give me a stone, please. Con Veile said the first stone had to be laid in the light, and the sun's half down.'

He stilled for a moment, and then trotted down to the stream to fetch her a washed stone. Round, red sandstone, worn smooth by the water. Red as her hair. Red as Queen Boudicca's hair. He helped her and Cram to rise. Oh, Mothers, her head hurt so badly when she moved! 'Cram – is there a prayer for this?'

Stern-faced in the growing dusk, Cram swayed and steadied. Berrin had brought him a stone, too, of glinting light grey, and a darker one for himself. 'I don't know. I've never buried a queen before.' He almost smiled. 'Trust the gods, this day of all days they'll forgive us if we make any mistakes.'

Victoria bent, her head spinning, and laid her stone on the turned earth. 'I start the cairn for Queen Boudicca.'

'For Boudicca, wife of Prasutaeg, daughter of Vaerana, daughter of Dourre, descended from Lugh of the sky.' Cram hissed in pain as he tossed his stone beside hers.

'For Queen Boudicca.' Berrin's voice was deep and dark.

A black stone thudded into the soft earth. 'For Boudicca, last queen of the Iceni.' Con Veile's voice hummed beside them. 'Let the queen's spirit go with the light, and rise again in joy in the Land of Youth. But let no other stones be laid on her. Let her grave go into the land unmarked, so that every hill in Britain may be the sacred place of her burial.'

The last sliver of sun disappeared behind the far-off hills. Below them, the Romans were remounting, calling farewells and promises to return. Berrin grunted in satisfaction. 'They've not taken my horses, just the old cart and its pair, to carry some of the young pigs, some hens and two – no, three goats. That Melissa, she's a good lass.'

'They'll be back.' Victoria grinned wryly as they stared at her. 'Ach, they're soldiers! A warm welcome, a pretty girl, good ale – she'll be running a tavern in ten days, and every legionary in Britain calling by.'

Berrin spat in disgust, but the druid shook her head at him. 'We must all stay for a while, Berrin,' she warned him. 'If as soon as we meet Romans we disappear, they might start wondering why, and ask awkward questions. Bring trouble on Melissa. And we all owe her too much to do that. Without her—'

'Aye.' He rubbed his head. 'No hardship, staying, I suppose. Not for a while. She'll need help with the brewing. I'll go home before the winter, though. By that time she'll have found another man. A Roman, likely. Or several . . . Ach, well.' He picked up his axe and spade and walked heavily off down the hill.

'I will leave also, fairly soon. An old woman will hardly be missed.' Con Veile considered the firelight glowing faintly from the open door below, and the light from the burning house across the fields. 'There will be many without hearths, without

200

roofs. I must try to help them. Preserve and rescue what I can. Rebuild after the Romans' vengeance. Share out what food there is – few villages sowed seed this year, thinking to live off the Romans.'

'Cheswell did. Boudicca persuaded my mother to insist on it. Another debt we owe her.' Cram sighed wearily. 'How long till my shoulder mends, druid?'

'Maybe two months. Less if you rest it, more if you try to work with it.'

'Then I'll wait to travel home until I can help Berrin with the horses. See if I can help my parents, my village. And then – go on with the fight. For the old days, the old ways! Con Veile, you saw even a mail shirt did not save Mac Clanna, when the god wanted him to die. But I suppose – yes, they are useful, for when the gods are not watching . . . You told Boudicca – Victoria – never to give up. No more will I. While the Romans stay on our land, they will fear the arrow in the forest, the poison in the well, the dagger in the dark.'

Victoria shivered at the grim bleakness of his voice and expression as he looked after the departing cavalrymen. 'I cannot fight, not in battle. But sing I can do. I can make songs, though I will never be trained in the druids' school. Many bards were travelling, and still live. I'll find them, learn from them. I'll sing for the Roman overlords, too. Could they ever suspect that the songs a crippled harper sings for coins to the rich and powerful might be different from those he sings to his friends, in private?

He glanced at the grave. 'A new harp I must make since Larksong is gone with the queen. I'll call her . . . Coronach. It is near enough a Latin word that they will believe it means Crown of Song; but the coronach is really the Deathsong . . . Will you help me, Con Veile?'

'With the harp, as far as my knowledge goes, and Berrin may know more. But after, with your work, no. I will rebuild, not add to the destruction. But you . . .' She shook her head sadly. 'I see you will not be changed. You have found your reason to go on, to live, until you die.'

His eyes were burning fierce with fanaticism. 'As all the gods see me, I swear. Until I die.'

The druid smiled gently at Victoria. 'You'll not stay here, though, Boudicca.'

Victoria looked round, slowly. 'No. What is there here for me? I'm like you, druid. I have no family or friends, except you and Melissa, and you will all have your own lives. No home, for I can't stay here. Rufius will see that I'm never accepted among the Romans, if he's still alive and comes back to Londinium – I've seen several people starting to rebuild there already, and he said he'd bought half the town, much good may it do him! And the Iceni will always reject me, though I am one by blood.' Cram nodded regretfully. 'I'm neither Roman nor Iceni. I'm not really Victoria Aegypta, nor Boudicca.' She shrugged. 'Besides, there is the geas the queen laid on me.'

'At heart you are Iceni, Boudicca,' Con Veile murmured. 'Or you'd not feel bound to obey the queen's sacred command.'

'Hah! Destroy Rome, destroy the Romans who destroy Britain! Me, one girl alone? Crazy. But . . . Somehow . . . It's only justice. I will do what I can. And I can't do anything against Rome, away out here, in the middle of a field at the far edge of the world. So, I must go away.'

'You will do it, if anyone can!' Cram took her hand. 'May the Three Mothers watch over you and protect you wherever you are, cousin. But where will you go?'

'First, over to my sister in Burdigala, and then to Massilia. Dio talked of a trainer there. Then maybe to Capua, where the best schools are, and then to Rome itself, I suppose.'

'A trainer?' He was puzzled. 'Schools? For what? What will you do?'

She drew her sword and held it out gleaming in the last of the light. Somehow Needle's sturdy, balanced weight, the reliable steel, the hint of gold, lifted her heart. This was something she knew, something she was good at. 'I may not be a noble warrior, but I'm a fighter. So that's what I'll do. Fight. I'll go into the arena, and win more glory and wealth than anyone ever has. I'll fight before the Emperor himself. Then let Rome beware, for I'll strike right at her heart as a gladiatrix.'

Glossary

Roman/Latin words are shown [L]

Celtic words are marked [C]

as [L]	copper coin (4 asses = 1 sesterce; a loaf cost 1 as)
bard	druid specialising in music; singer, harpist
Bridhe [C]	maiden goddess of spring, youth, hope
Brigantes [L]	Roman name for British tribe
Burdigala [L]	Bordeaux, in France
Cailleach (the) [C]	old woman, goddess of winter, age, wisdom
Camulodunum [L]	Colchester
Catuvellauni [L]	Roman name for British tribe
centurion [L]	under-officer in charge of a century (= staff-sergeant)
century [L]	army unit, about 80/100 men (6 centuries = 1 cohort)
Cernunnos [C]	nature god, god of harvest

cohort [L]	army unit, about 500 men (10 cohorts = 1 legion)
decurion [L]	under-officer in charge of about 10 men, especially cavalry (= corporal)
Deva [L]	Chester
druid [C]	Celtic professional priest, doctor, teacher, judge, etc.
geas [C]	commandment from the gods; breaking it meant death
governor [L]	chief Roman officer and official of a province, e.g. Britain
Herne [C]	nature god, god of hunting
Iceni [L]	Roman name for British tribe
Isca Dumnoniorum [L]	Exeter
legate [L]	officer commanding a legion
legion [L]	regiment; officially about 5,500 men, including 120 cavalry and about 400 auxiliaries (often non-Roman specialists, boatmen, slingers, archers, etc.)
Lindum [L]	Lincoln
Londinium [L]	London
Lugh [C]	sun god, god of light and air
Macha [C]	mature goddess of summer, fertility, motherhood

Mars [L]	god of war; Mars Ultor – Avenging Mars, who always strikes the final, winning blow
Massilia [L]	Marseilles, in France
Mona [C]	Anglesey
Morrigan (the) [C]	goddess of destruction
nemet [C]	sacred grove of trees, usually oak; equivalent to a church
optio [L]	second-in-command to a centurion
ovate [C]	druid specialising in foretelling the future or speaking with the dead
procurator [L]	Roman official in conquered countries, in charge of money, taxes, coinage, trade deals
senator [L]	member of Roman Senate, or Parliament
sesterce [L]	small silver coin
sounder	family group of wild pigs
thane	headman of a town; baron
torc [C]	neck ornament, open C-ring of twisted gold or silver wires
tribune [L]	young officer assisting legate, general or other official; often commanding a cohort

Trinovantes [L]	Roman name for British tribe
Venta Icenorum [L]	Roman name of Caistor, by Norwich; main town of Iceni
Verulamium [L]	St Albans
Viroconium [L]	Wroxeter

Find out what happens to Victoria next in the second book of the Gladiatrix trilogy: *Victrix* – publishing soon. Here's a taster . . .

'Sir?'

The speaker was as tall as Victoria, dark curls glossy in the sunlight. His shockingly short leopard-skin tunic left long legs, a sleekly muscled bronzed torso and one broad shoulder gleaming in the morning sun. She almost smirked. Didn't he think he was something! She despised handsome, conceited men.

Then her breathing caught as she saw his face. Something had sliced twice, right across his face. One hideous scar ran from his left temple, across his eyebrow, twisting it askew; then across the bridge of his nose and down his right cheek. The other ran from his left cheekbone across his mouth, distorting his lips into a permanent bitter half-smile. Imprisoned in this wrecked cage, intelligent dark-brown eyes gleamed alert for her reaction.

'Ah, Pulcher. A volunteer, Victoria,' Glaevius introduced her. 'Try her out.'

Pulcher meant Beautiful. Who named him that, in jeering ridicule or irony? Older than herself, but not yet thirty. What a tragedy for him! But he defied his fate, wearing that extravagantly showy tunic that would make an actor blush, ironically drawing attention to himself. Had she shown shock? She hoped not. It would hurt so badly.

Pulcher was studying her. 'You want to be a gladiatrix?'

She straightened self-consciously, dragging her gaze to meet his eyes. 'Yes, sir.'

'Hmm.' He walked round her, considering her. 'Strip.'

'Strip? Here – in front of all these . . . ?'

'If you want to join them, you join them. Worse will happen to you than embarrassment, girl. If you can't take it, the gate is behind you, leave while you can.'

Behind her the clacking thuds and shouting were fading. Everyone was stopping to stare. Pulcher gazed round sardonically. 'Rest time already?' The noise rose again.

Victoria's temper started to simmer, but she fought it down. This man would be in charge of her training. True, she had to do what the rest did – and he wasn't making her a show just for fun.

This morning she had carefully wrapped up nose to toes like a decent Roman girl, only her face peering from the shapeless cocoon of dark blue wool. She loosened her wrap round her shoulders, and drew a deep, trembling breath. Right. She had planned and practised this; now to see if it worked.

She spun, whirling the cloth flying above her like a banner. Under it she wore her brightest Iceni clothes; red checked shirt, yellow-and-black striped trousers, blue leather jerkin and sandals. Her sword, Needle, was slung in front of her waist, to hang unnoticed between her knees if she sat down. She drew it and brandished it high, shrieking a war-cry that stilled the yard to sudden silence. Glaevius and Pulcher both leapt away in swift reaction as, in one second, she turned from a big, lumpy, respectable girl into a warrior of the Iceni ready for battle, the shocking swirl of tattoos on her scalp blazing across the exercise yard.

Fine so far. What next? Keep going? Keep going!

Victoria stuck her sword point into a trestle and set her hands on her belt buckle, grinning defiantly. 'You want me to go right down?'

From all round arose a chorus of whistles, laughter and clapping. Even Glaevius's lips twitched.

Pulcher's didn't. 'What do you think this is, a pantomime?' He glanced round; training recommenced at once.

'I wondered why you were sweltering like that.' Glaevius eyed her head with interest. 'Hmm. You realise that half the show is showmanship. Good.'

Pulcher nodded towards the sword. 'Can you use that?'

She grinned tightly. 'How hard can it be? You stick the pointy end in.'

He didn't laugh. He sighed. 'Another smart-arse.'

She glared. 'I've killed my man.' More than one, in fact, but she didn't want to talk about it.

Neither did he. He didn't look impressed as she had hoped; he sneered. 'That means you've a load of bad habits that we'll have to train out of you. Like that sword. We don't use steel here. Not for training. Nor keep it in the barracks, not with slaves about.'

She bristled. 'I don't give Needle up for anyone!'

'It has a name? A real barbarian trick! Then leave,' he challenged her, raising an eyebrow towards Glaevius, who nodded.

What? Losing Needle would be like losing an arm! But if it was the only way . . . 'All right.'

Glaevius grunted satisfaction. 'Yes, you are determined. Do not worry, I shall keep it safe for you. You might even use it in the ring.'

As Victoria's face cleared, Pulcher jerked his head disdainfully at her. 'Let's see if you fight as well as you act.'

Victoria laid her scabbard and wrap on the trestle beside Needle. The noise was dying again – the men were stopping training, to spectate. This time Pulcher allowed it. She glanced round at the grins, the expectant eyes. They wanted a show? She'd show them!

In the open square in the middle the fighters stood aside. One offered her his wooden sword and small shield.

'Ready?' Suddenly Pulcher's wooden sword smacked her left arm. She cursed indignantly, and then was being chased all over the palaestra. Pulcher was fast, stabbing, weaving, driving her among the posts. The other men leapt clear, cheering and jeering. Curse him, curse this curved sword, it was oddly balanced, the shield was too small, he was making her look like

212

a fool! She ducked round a post from one side to the other, left, right, left, suddenly doubled back, parried a blow harder than he had expected, and thrust in return. He jumped back, and for a minute they exchanged blows. She was getting used to the sword – he dropped back, she advanced gleefully, got him on the run –

Her sword suddenly jolted out of her grasp, flying away to clatter against the wall on the far side of the yard. She cursed again as Pulcher's blade whacked her bottom, and the crowd jeered. But then he nodded, lips twisted derisively. 'I suppose my old granny would do worse.'

Not panting, he led her back towards Glaevius. 'Fairly fit, not bad balance. Her wrist's strong, her eye's straight, quick reactions, and she's not shy of being hit. She's been taught a bit, by a cavalryman, and she's used to fighting longer weapons, spears maybe, or long Gaulish swords. Her knees are stiff. No idea about using a shield, and the left hand is very weak. But she learns fast.' He shrugged. 'Worth a try, if Manny can fix the hand.'

'How could you tell all that?' she demanded. 'About the cavalryman?'

Glaevius smiled slightly. 'He has fought in the arena for thirteen years, girl. There is little he cannot tell about an opponent after one minute. If he says you are worth training—'

'You'll take me on?' Her grin was ecstatic. She turned it on Pulcher. 'Oh, thank you!'

He shrugged a dismissive shoulder. 'Thank me again next year – if you're still alive.'